Cover art by Brenda Walter
Editing by Heather Hayden
Narration by Jay

This is a work of fiction. Similarities to real people, places, or events are entirely coincidental.

A SECRET BABY IN THE SHOW ME STATE

First edition. July 2, 2020.

Copyright © 2020 Jessie Gussman.

Written by Jessie Gussman.

Dedication

To Mr. Heinrich and his late, beautiful wife, Miss Sally.

As an author, I've had the opportunity to meet the most amazing people. I've had great conversations and have grown to love many of them. Mr. Heinrich is one of those people.

The idea for this book – a baby abandoned next to a man in a church with just a note - came directly from Mr. Heinrich. I'm grateful and blessed, not just that he had an idea and entrusted me with it, but also for his words of wisdom, his timely Bible verses, his quirky questions (why do women seem to tuck their legs under them while they sit, but men do not?) and most of all, for the beautiful and inspiring stories of his late wife, Miss Sally. Miss Sally was exactly the kind of Christian that I hope to someday be. I think it is a beautiful testimony of the kind of person that she was that she is still influencing other women, who have never met her, to live for the Lord from beyond the grave. She is a role-model for me.

Prologue

Deacon Hudson knelt at the pew in the last row of the little country church in Cowboy Crossing, Missouri, praying. His forehead rested on his hands, and he whispered his words to the Almighty.

Around him came footsteps and a low murmur of voices as pastors who had gathered to question him at his ordination talked among themselves quietly, being respectful of his kneeling position and current occupation.

Today represented the day he'd looked forward to all his life. It had been his dream ever since he could remember to become a pastor and preach the Word of God. To share the Gospel of Christ, comforting people, exhorting them to good works, and hopefully leading the small flock in his own hometown.

The pastors assembled had already read and researched about him, interviewing family and friends and neighbors.

Today, they would ask him questions, and barring a major surprise, he would be ordained as a pastor of God's Word.

"I've never met anyone more qualified than Deacon." A voice spoke softly toward the front of the church, interrupting Deacon's conversation with the Lord.

"We couldn't find anyone who had one bad thing to say about him. His doctrine and faith have been solid all his life. He never even went astray as a teenager."

Deacon tried to shut the words out and concentrate on his humble supplication to his Creator. Those men might think it was a given, and maybe it was, but he wasn't any better than anybody else, never had been. Sure, maybe he hadn't done some of the bad things that other people had done, but he was still just a wretched sinner, undeserving to represent the Lord in any way. And yet here God was, opening this door for him for this position that he'd felt called to since he was a child.

Funny how the timelines matched, or maybe not so funny, because it was obviously God's working. The church needed a pastor just at the time that he completed his training and college courses and was ready to be ordained.

He could preach without being ordained, although most churches required it of their pastor, but he couldn't marry or bury anyone.

With the humblest of hearts, and a body bursting with gratefulness, he begged the Lord to give him wisdom like Solomon. Wisdom to lead God's people and walk the path that God had for him. To do right, no matter how tempting it was to do what he wanted.

His lips moved as the soft words fell from them.

It was almost time. He could tell because all the sounds were coming from the front now.

Except one. The door opened. It must be a late arrival.

Was that a baby's cry? Odd.

He wasn't exactly an expert on children, although he'd been around them some. The sound came again. Yeah, he was pretty sure that was a baby fussing.

Still, he wasn't quite finished and didn't lift his head even when the footsteps stopped beside him, and it sounded like something was being set down.

He finished the sentence he'd been saying and raised his face just in time to see a figure walk behind the pew.

He didn't look long, because another sound came from beside him.

His eyes shifted. Definitely a baby.

Surprise stretched his features, although he stayed on his knees. He cut his eyes back to the person—man? Woman? He wasn't sure—just in time to see them disappear. The click of the heavy wooden door echoed in the now quiet sanctuary.

Deacon stood, his eyes bouncing from the baby that lay in the car seat in the aisle beside his pew, around the sanctuary, to the group of men whose every eye was either on him or the baby, and back to the baby.

Growing up on a farm in south-central Missouri, he'd had a lot of crazy things happen to him. A lot of it had to do with the weather. Fires, tornadoes, windstorms. Flash floods. There were other odd experiences too, some with animals and some with machinery.

There were a lot of crazy people running around as well. Crazy to the rest of the world, maybe, but normal to a Missourian. They grew them tough in this state. Hardy. And they were proud of it.

But he had to admit this was a first, even for the craziness of the Show Me state.

A baby? Someone just left a baby. Walked away from it. Without saying anything.

Only a few seconds passed, and he became aware of a fluorescent pink piece of paper stuck to where the baby's feet probably were under the swaddling blanket that was tucked around it.

The word swaddling came to his head, not because of any experience with babies but because of Mary wrapping Jesus in swaddling clothes in the Bible. A passage he was most definitely familiar with. Unlike babies.

If he had to guess though, he'd say it was a pretty young one. It was small anyway and didn't seem to be able to hold its head up, since it tilted to the side. The little eyes were squinted and wrinkled, and he couldn't really tell if they were open or shut. The mouth was tiny and bow shaped. The infant wore a thin pink hat.

A girl?

Deacon looked around again: still no one in the sanctuary except the men who were about to question him. Several of them stood at the front, frozen in the act of walking toward him. As though they were waiting to see what he would do.

What should he do? The baby wasn't his. He knew that for a fact. He might be going to be ordained today, but he still knew the facts of life.

He knew the facts but didn't have the actual experience, because as the Bible commanded, he was waiting for his marriage.

Not that there was any marriage in the foreseeable future, since girls weren't the species that he typically hung around.

There'd been one, back in high school, he'd been interested in, but she ran with the popular crowd and certainly wasn't the slightest bit into him.

God would provide a wife. He just had to be patient.

He sighed and stepped out of the pew, his eyes on the note.

Footsteps came behind him, but he didn't turn his head to look. Instead, he bent down and picked up the note, straightening as he read it.

Deacon Hudson is the father. Take care of her.

The only other word on the note was "Tinsley." He wasn't sure whether that was the baby's name or the signature of the person who wrote it.

There was a pink flowered bag beside the car seat—a baby bag?—that he just noticed, and a little pack of papers stuck out of the side pocket. Maybe they would shed more light on the situation.

Before he could bend over, a deep voice from behind him said, "Does that note say that the baby is yours?" The voice held inquiry but also sounded a little shocked.

It snapped Deacon out of his contemplative daze, and the implications of what the note said and everything it seemed to mean hit him hard.

He dropped to his knees, which was how he handled almost every problem, but he didn't have the luxury of more than a bullet prayer right now. Pulling the pack of papers out of the little bag, he stood back up, his heart still crying out to the Lord.

What is the meaning of this, God? You know this could ruin everything.

His heart cried and railed more, but outwardly he managed to keep his calm demeanor as he held the papers—a birth certificate, maybe?—and handed the note to a rough, gnarled hand that stretched out for it.

He had nothing to hide. Nothing. This baby was not his, and it was on the tip of his tongue to say so as he opened the pack of papers and pulled out one that said "Official Record of Birth" at the top of it.

His eyes scanned across the official print, easily catching his name on the line that said "father."

His breath caught. His mind screamed. The paper in his hand bent and crackled as his fingers clenched.

If he'd been alone, he'd be on his knees with both fists raised and shaking at the sky.

Why, God? Why now, when everything was falling into place? Why are You allowing this to happen?

No one would ever believe the baby wasn't his. Everyone in this room would think that he'd lied to them about his past. In their eyes, the "fact" that he had a child was just as damning as the "fact" that he'd lied about it or, at the very least, hidden it.

If he didn't straighten this up, insist on his innocence, deny, and defend, starting right now, he could kiss his ordination goodbye.

Anger rose, hot and fierce, in his chest at the person who would do this to him. He scanned the birth certificate again. Under mother's name, it said: RECORD CLOSED.

He would fight. This would not keep him from being ordained. He would win and become a pastor.

Probably not today.

Above the fierce beating of his heart and the gasping of his breath and the whirling of his blood in his veins as his soul cried and begged God to fix this and not let it keep him from succeeding in everything that he'd worked for and strived for and wanted all his life, a still, quiet voice, almost audible, seemed to whisper in his ear.

My plan, not yours.

No, God. Please, no. I want to be a pastor. I want to preach Your word, feed Your sheep, shepherd Your flock. Let me do what I want.

Surrender. Submit. If you love Me, obey.

Chapter 1

Seven years later

"I know six kids are a lot, and I appreciate you meeting with me anyway. Even if Lynette did twist your arm to get you to do it."

Deacon gave the woman sitting in front of him a kind smile. He hoped it was kind anyway. It was true that Lynette had twisted his arm. Admitting that would only hurt Inez's feelings.

Inez Cromwell would make any man a good wife. She'd been faithful and true to her husband, despite the fact that the man had been...not nice.

"Lynette has a lot of good advice, and she also has a way of seeing things that make sense after you think about it. I'd have been a fool to not listen to her."

He believed that. Even if he wasn't very happy about it. It wasn't that he didn't want six children—it would be seven if one added Tinsley to the mix.

He just didn't feel attraction for Inez. He liked to talk to her okay. She was a nice lady, and he figured they could probably rub along okay even if she were four years older than he. That didn't matter either.

He just wasn't sure if he was old enough, at thirty, to settle for someone that he liked but didn't love. At least not in the way the world defined love.

Is it wrong for me to want a fire, Lord?

An attraction. He wanted an attraction and maybe even the feeling that he couldn't keep his hands off his wife. He supposed, with six children already, it was probably best if there were no powerful drives or attraction.

I've waited, Lord. This is really what I get? A lukewarm liking? It's not fair to her either.

Inez had suffered through a horrible marriage to a man who had been unkind and didn't appreciate her. She'd found his dead body in the shower last fall, shortly before Thanksgiving, leaving her a widow with six children to raise. Only the baking business that she had done on the side supported them.

Her life hadn't been easy. She deserved a man who would love her passionately, with his whole soul. Who would admire her and respect her and need her to make him complete.

Did God not have such a man for her?

And such a woman for Deacon?

He would never voice his questions aloud; they were private between the Lord and himself.

Inez spoke a little more about her children and family and what their routines were. He supposed if they decided to get together, he'd need to know.

He liked children. Loved Tinsley and could see himself falling for Inez's. He knew them from church, and they were good kids.

It wasn't the kids.

Deacon leaned toward Inez just a little, to let her know he was listening, but his eyes went to the playground where Tinsley played with Inez's children. A couple of them were older, and four of them were younger. Tinsley would fit in just fine. In fact, he'd often wished that she'd had siblings to grow up with, although she had cousins she was close to, so it was almost the same. Still, she would love to be a part of a big active household.

They were playing some kind of tag on the monkey bars, chasing each other. Tinsley kept up with the other kids. He was proud of her for holding her own, even though this wasn't something that was completely familiar to her.

He'd done the best he could as a single father. His mother helped a lot, because after he wasn't ordained, the church in Cowboy Crossing had hired Lynette's husband, Pastor Wyatt, and Deacon had slid rather easily into the role of unpaid assistant pastor. The unpaid part of that was fine with Deacon, because he felt like he was working for the Lord, and God paid better than anyone else. But it wasn't earthly payment, so Deacon also worked a "real" job.

He had a small farm, which paid most of the bills, and he worked at the fertilizer plant on the side.

"They get along well, don't they?" Inez's voice was soft and sweet, and he didn't think it was a put-on act. Her personality was calm, and after being married to Mr. Cromwell, she exemplified long-suffering.

If he was to get married to her, she wouldn't have to suffer long in their marriage. He sure hoped he was a step up from Mr. Cromwell.

Miss Lynette wanted them to—it was the reason she had set up this meeting between them, without making any bones about it. She'd laughed and said, "How could I not? Two unmarried people in the church who are perfect for each other. Just give it a try."

Deacon didn't even want to take Inez's hand. She reminded him more of his mother, despite the fact that they were only a few years apart. Not her fault, it was just the way he felt.

He wanted to be married. True. He wanted a helper who would stand beside him, a companion, friend, and lover. He wanted all of that.

But he wasn't sure he wanted it with Inez, whom he still thought of most of the time as Mrs. Cromwell.

One of her younger children, a little boy, Richard, fell off the seesaw and started to cry.

"Oh, excuse me, please," Inez said as she got up and hurried over to the playground. She wore capris, and Deacon couldn't fault her figure. Sure, it wasn't young-girl slim, but he wasn't looking for a young girl. That didn't appeal to him either.

He wanted to growl in frustration. Maybe there was something wrong with him.

Ever since he'd gotten Tinsley, he hadn't even tried to date, not that he'd done it much before, either, because he'd been so consumed with Bible college, mission trips, and getting ordained.

Mrs. Cromwell picked her child up and carried Richard back, sitting down on the bench beside Deacon, a little closer than she'd been before. He doubted it was on purpose though. Richard was a hefty little boy and probably heavy.

His crying made talking impossible, so Deacon tried to shove his morose thoughts aside and smiled as Tinsley and the Cromwell children competed to see who could swing the highest.

This evening, he'd not gone visiting like he usually did, wearing his hat of assistant pastor. But he would make that up tomorrow. Mrs. Cromwell couldn't meet tomorrow, since she had baking to do for the weekend for her baked goods business.

A blue truck, slightly old and beat-up, but not as much as Ivory's—Ivory being his brother's fiancée—rumbled down the street.

Cowboy Crossing wasn't a huge town. He recognized most vehicles and could give a first name or last name of the driver or someone associated with it. It was the kind of town where everybody knew everybody.

That's what made the truck stick out. The dents and faded paint declared it a working truck, but he knew all the farmers in the area, and it didn't belong to any of them.

He watched as it pulled further down the street and parked in front of Mrs. Dixon's house. The person inside wore a cowboy hat, so Deacon didn't have a hope of recognizing them until they got out.

It was a woman.

Slim jeans and a tank top. Cowboy boots.

Inez should be more his style, but his eyes wanted to linger on the woman across the street. She grabbed a bag from the passenger seat, slung it over her shoulder, and slammed the door shut. The latch didn't catch the first time.

Almost as though she expected it, she was ready to slam again harder the second time. It caught, and the woman slapped the top of the old beat-up toolbox in the bed of the truck as she walked with long confident strides around the back of the truck and up onto Mrs. Dixon's porch.

Deacon's heart stuttered.

Mrs. Dixon was on his list of people to visit tomorrow. He visited her every week. She was young—just in her fifties—but was laid up with MS. It was getting worse.

That wasn't what caused his heart stutter.

Mrs. Dixon was Blair Dixon's mother. In high school, Blair was a cheerleader who hung with the popular crowd.

He, along with every other male in her vicinity, had a crush on her. Nothing major, because even at that age, he knew nothing could ever come of it. She wasn't the kind of girl who was going to marry a preacher and farmer and stay in town.

He did wonder what happened to her though, because he'd had a conversation with her two years after she graduated.

It was the only time he ever felt like he was on equal footing with her, that day when they talked.

He couldn't forget their last conversation, because she'd been in trouble. She'd been going down a bad road, knew it, but didn't know how to get herself straightened out.

She hadn't been living in town, but had been visiting and sought him out, like a lot of people did, because he was working on his pastor's degree and she needed counseling.

If he had to do it again, he might have recused himself and told her to talk to someone else. There were no written rules, but he was pretty sure he shouldn't be attracted to the people he was counseling.

He also shouldn't have agreed to meet her at midnight…but he had.

There wouldn't have been a second session. But he hadn't had to turn her down, because she never called him again.

Her truck wasn't in the best shape, but she looked good, and he was happy that she'd apparently got her life straightened out.

"I think that might have been Blair Dixon." Inez's voice came from beside him, and he startled guiltily. It wouldn't do to get married, be sitting beside his wife, and be thinking about another woman.

Deacon turned to look at her. Inez didn't have any accusation on her face, just polite conversation.

If she were attracted to him, if she really wanted him, and wasn't just meeting him because Lynette wanted her to, wouldn't she be a little jealous? Wouldn't she have noticed that his eyes were tracking Blair as she got out of her truck and walked into her house? Would it occur to her that he stared at the Dixons' door long after it closed and that was a little unusual?

He didn't think Inez was into him. Any more than he was into her.

Chapter 2

Blair Dixon stirred the eggs on the stove. Her mom had been worse than she expected when she had arrived yesterday afternoon.

She'd been well enough to put up a social media post announcing that her daughter was back. But her motor coordination wasn't good.

And her mother never slept in this late.

In all the years that she'd spent growing up in this small town, her mom had been an early riser, always the first to have her laundry on the line.

The only one to have her laundry on the line.

Even though her mom lived in town, she loved baking and canning and everything that had to do with rural life. All of which involved getting up at some insane hour of the morning. Before daylight, usually.

Blair checked her phone: three minutes later than it was last time she checked. Nine thirty-two.

She flipped the eggs and added cheese before getting out a plate.

Rascal, her mom's little dog, some kind of mix she got at the pound, whined at her feet.

"No. These are for Mom. Let me see if I can find your food." She rooted around some until she finally found a small bag of dog food and filled up Rascal's bowl. She had already taken Rascal outside for a short walk, and the water bowl was still half full of clean water.

Biting her lip, she looked at the plate. Should she take it up to her mom? And if her mom slept in this late now, what had she been doing before Blair arrived? Who had been taking care of her?

Maybe she was just having a really bad day.

Guilt threatened to clutch the back of her neck, and she pushed it aside. She couldn't spend the rest of her life feeling guilty about the stupid decisions she made when she was a kid. All she could do was work to unravel them.

And now she'd be working on them back here in her hometown, which was harder because everyone knew what she'd done, although there was one thing they didn't know.

She took the stairs two at a time, always running. It was something she'd started doing after she got out. It helped calm her stress levels and made her feel a little free.

"Mom!" she called as she reached the top. The bathroom door was cracked, and the light was off, so she assumed her mom was still in her room.

"Mom?" she said as she walked down the hall to the back bedroom. Still no answer.

She tapped on the door softly. "Mom?"

There was a rustling, and a little creak, and then her mom's voice. "Blair?" Just a thread of sound. "You can come in. The door's unlocked."

She cracked the door, pushing it open slowly. "Mom? It's nine thirty. Are you okay?"

Her mom put a hand to her head, almost like it hurt. The blinds were drawn; the room was dark. It almost looked like it was still the middle of the night in there. "Is it that late? I guess I just didn't sleep very well last night."

A little shot of fear went through Blair's chest. She hadn't been a very good daughter. She'd caused her mom a lot of stress and care and worry.

When she saw her mom like this, it was harder to push the guilt away, but she did it anyway. She couldn't change the past. She could only make sure the future didn't repeat it.

"Do you feel like getting up? I can help you." She added that last sentence, not really thinking that her mom would take her up on it.

"Thank you. If you wouldn't mind, I'll take your arm. Sometimes standing first thing in the morning is hard."

Blair blinked several times. She hadn't been expecting that. Didn't want to hear it. But that didn't mean she could ignore it.

"Sure. Just tell me what to do."

Her mom let out a deep, long-suffering sigh. "I'm so glad you're here. I was almost at the point where I couldn't do things myself anymore."

Blair had noticed yesterday that she seemed a lot slimmer, seemed to have lost a lot of weight, but she had attributed it to the fact that her mom had said she was trying to eat healthier. Maybe it was because her mom hadn't been able to feed herself or cook for herself.

"Some days are better than others," her mom said, as though she could read her mind. "This is one of the bad ones. I try to get the grocery shopping and other errands done on the days where I feel good."

Blair nodded. It was just so unlike her mother to not be spry and involved and ready to take on the world. She'd always been energetic and constantly volunteering, especially at the church, where she taught Sunday school and helped with Bible school and taught the kids' club on Wednesday night and organized fruit baskets and meals for new mothers. There was no end to the list of things her mom had done, along with her full-time job as a receptionist at the animal hospital in nearby Trumbull.

This version of her mother who could hardly get out of bed was startling. It hadn't been that long since she'd visited. Only three months.

It took them two hours, but she was able to get her mother showered and fed breakfast. She'd helped her pay some bills, writing out the checks and having her mother sign them, since her mother's fingers weren't working very well with the pen.

After that, her mom had been exhausted and was now upstairs resting.

Blair had gone outside to sit on the back steps, watching Rascal jump and play in the big backyard. The one she'd played in when she was younger. The swing set and inflatable swimming pool were long gone, but she had a lot of good memories from back there.

No siblings. Just didn't happen. Her dad was in and out, and her mom never remarried after he left for good.

Blair had thought her move would be temporary, and she would kill two birds with one stone. She had something she needed to fix. Something that stemmed from her past and had ruined someone's life. Maybe not ruined it, exactly, but had destroyed his dream. She didn't know if she could fix that or not. But she could at least see if she could try to set it right, although she had no idea how. Just a nagging guilt and longing.

She intended to help her mom too. But it looked like her mom needed a caregiver full-time.

There was no reason why Blair couldn't come back and live in Cowboy Crossing. Except she would never escape her reputation. She wanted to go somewhere and be someone new, instead of having to live with all the old things she'd done.

It took about two seconds to destroy a good reputation. And two lifetimes to rebuild a bad one. It would be easier to do it somewhere else, which was what she'd been working on.

She didn't know how long she'd sat there thinking, trying to figure out what to do, trying not to think about her mother and the things she couldn't do anymore, because if she did her eyes pricked and her throat clogged up and it wouldn't be long until she was crying. It was the middle of the day; she couldn't afford to cry.

The doorbell chimed faintly through the screen door, and Blair stood up. Who would be ringing the doorbell at this hour? She grabbed her phone and checked the time. One o'clock. She hadn't realized how late it was getting to be.

Sitting around moping wasn't something she normally indulged in. She'd need to get serious about finding some work, if she were going to stay. She wasn't going to bum off her mother.

Calling Rascal, she walked in the back door and went through the house to the front. Blair opened it, not knowing what to expect. Her mother hadn't said anything about anyone visiting.

It took her about half a second to recognize the man standing in front of her. For another half a second, she had about a million thoughts go through her brain—most of them worst-case scenarios, because she thought he was here for her and had figured out what she'd done. But it didn't even take another half second to dismiss that thought from her head. If he'd figured out what she'd done, he would have looked her up long before this. It wasn't like everybody didn't know everybody else's business in this small town.

Deacon would know about her prison record.

"Hello, Blair," he said. "Saw your pickup pull in yesterday. Was surprised to see it today yet. I didn't figure you'd still be here."

She nodded. Where had he been that he'd seen her pickup? Last she heard, his spread was outside of town next to Wilder Stryker's and Deacon's parents'.

A small place if she remembered correctly from what her mom said.

She always paid attention when her mom talked about Deacon, which wasn't that often.

He kept standing there, and her mouth started moving. "I was planning on being here for a while, but I might stay permanently. My mom's a lot worse than what she was last time I was here early this spring."

Deacon nodded, like they talked all the time. "It does seem like things are progressing rapidly. From what I understand, though, that's the nature of the disease. She might hit another plateau soon."

He shifted, and she realized he was wearing a pair of dark jeans and a nice button-down. One that was clean and new and said good clothes. Going-to-visit clothes.

The shoulders were broader than she remembered, although he was just as slim. Maybe a little taller. His face looked a little more rugged, and she'd definitely call him handsome. She remembered his hair as being a little lighter too. Now, it was a golden brown rather than a golden blond.

His eyes were still kind and serious. They still seemed to see way more than anyone else ever tried to. That's always the way she felt when he looked at her. That hadn't changed.

Nor had the little stirring in her chest and the quiet buzz that hummed just under her collarbone when he was around, ticking up a few notches when their eyes met.

It had always been that way. She wasn't quite sure what it was about him, but she felt that way every time. With another man, she might have called it attraction. With Deacon, she wasn't sure what to call it.

She cleared her throat while her cheeks heated. "I'm sorry. You can come in. Did you come to visit?" She stumbled over that last sentence a little, not sure why she even asked, except he looked like he was dressed for a visit.

"Yeah. I usually come to see your mom on Thursdays, but I was busy last night. So I came as soon as I got off work today."

She squinted her eyes and shook her head. "You're visiting my mom?"

He'd walked two steps in and stood, waiting while she shut the door, turned around, and looked at him. He stuck one hand in his pocket, and the other one hung loosely aside, the long brown fingers a little at odds with the nice clothes.

He nodded, his expression not changing and his eyes still giving her that deep, penetrating look that made her want to squirm. "I help Pastor Wyatt out. I often fill the duties of assistant pastor. It's an unpaid position. No one makes me do anything, but Pastor and I have an understanding. I do a lot of visiting for him."

Ouch. That hurt. She might not have been in town, but she knew exactly why Deacon Hudson wasn't the pastor of the Cowboy Crossing church. It had everything to do with her and what she'd selfishly wanted for her child.

She'd gotten it. In return, she stayed completely out of her daughter's life. The longing to see her child and be a mom had never gone away. She considered it part of her punishment. For being stupid. Stupid tax if one would. She'd be paying it for the rest of her life.

Although, some things were going to change. She didn't know how, exactly. But she had to undo the wrong she'd done to Deacon.

She picked at the material of her jeans, pushing words through her tight throat. "I'm sorry. She's sleeping right now. I guess today is one of her bad days. That's what she said, anyway. I haven't been around enough to know for sure if that's true."

She didn't mean to imply her mom might lie, but even though she hadn't been visiting, she talked to her mom almost every day. She'd never mentioned any of the many issues that Blair had seen just in the two hours that she'd spent with her this morning.

She supposed yesterday hadn't been much better, but she had assumed that her mom was overtired like she'd said. Before Blair arrived, she'd been outside weeding in the garden flowerbeds.

Deacon tapped his cowboy hat against his leg. "I can come back. She has my number, and you can give me a call when she's ready for me to come. I have some other visits I need to make."

Blair nodded. Normally, she didn't have trouble finding her tongue and making small talk, but Deacon wasn't like the other men that she knew. He never had been.

He didn't make any move to leave, though, continuing to look at her. "You staying for a while?"

Her heart beat a little faster, but she tried to hold it back. He was just making conversation typical of small towns, where everybody's business was anybody's business.

"I might be."

That was rude. Her mom would say she hadn't used her manners. She tried to pull herself together.

"Would you like to come on in to the kitchen? I can get you something to drink. Coffee, tea, water, or milk."

His head started to shake, but then they heard a creak upstairs and what sounded like slow footsteps from the ceiling above them.

"That might be Mom. You go on in to the kitchen, and I'll run upstairs and check." Funny, she didn't want to talk to him, but she didn't want him to leave either. Sometimes she was such an idiot. What did she want to do? Stand there and stare at him?

"Sure. I have all afternoon." He pulled his hand out of his pocket and strode down the hall toward the kitchen while she took the stairs two at a time and walked to her mother's room.

Rapping on the door lightly, she called, "Mom?"

"Did I hear voices down there?" Her mom's voice sounded stronger than it had this morning, even through the door.

"Deacon Hudson is down there to see you."

"I can't hear you. Open the door and come in."

She opened the door. Her mom sat on the edge of the bed, her feet on the floor, her hands placed on either side of her like she was gathering herself to stand up.

Blair closed the door behind her and walked over. "I said Deacon Hudson is downstairs. He's here to visit you."

Her mother's eyes brightened. Everyone in town had always liked Deacon—well-liked and well-respected. Even though he hadn't been ordained because of what she'd done to him, he could still have had the church in Cowboy Crossing if he'd chosen to. But her mom had told her later Deacon wouldn't take it because he wouldn't be a pastor who couldn't perform official ceremonies. He didn't feel like it was fair to the town.

When he finally was ordained, years later, the current pastor, Pastor Wyatt, was well-loved and permanent.

It added to her guilt. Constant guilt.

She hadn't been able to do anything about it, because she'd been in prison. She certainly hadn't realized when she'd paid one of her friends, who needed drug money, to help her that her daughter would be delivered to Deacon at the church, just before his ordination.

She walked over and held her hands out. "Can I help you?"

"Sure. Grip my elbows like you did before."

It felt a little less awkward this time, but it was still a position and movements she wasn't used to.

"I can get it from here, honey. Did you get him something to eat? And drink?"

"No. I didn't have a chance." That wasn't quite true. She'd been too busy standing in the middle of the floor feeling awkward.

"You go on down, then. Make him comfortable. I'll be down in a few minutes once I take care of some things."

"Are you sure you'll be okay?"

"I said I would." Her mom lifted her chin and jerked it. "Go on."

She had to go down and face Deacon again. She might as well get used to it. If he visited every week, she was bound to see him more. If he was the assistant pastor of the church, she'd see him then, too. Her mom would have to be dead before she wouldn't go to church.

If Blair were going to be in Cowboy Crossing, she'd need to be able to act normally with Deacon.

Although, after she admitted what she'd done, she might not be able to stay. He would hate her.

Maybe Deacon was too good for hate. Maybe he'd resent her instead.

Taking a deep, fortifying breath, she went down the stairs two at a time and hurried back to the kitchen.

Deacon stood at the back door, his arm braced against the jamb, staring out the window at the backyard. He turned as she approached.

His hat hung over the back of one of the chairs, and he hadn't helped himself to any drinks.

"She's on her way down." She put her hand on the chair beside Deacon's hat, trying to keep her lungs from pumping in and out. Going down the stairs shouldn't have caused her to be out of breath. She gulped in air. "She heard us down here talking. Her eyes really lit up when I told her you were here. I guess she likes you."

He grinned, and her eyes went to the cleft in his chin.

"Good to hear. Guess that's part of my job. Nice to know I'm successful with at least one person."

His words didn't sound like he was fishing for a compliment. They didn't sound like he was putting himself down either. Just like he was stating a fact.

She brushed her hands down her jeans and walked to the cupboard. She'd done some pretty hard things in her life and could see the humor that this cowboy from small-town Missouri was making her palms sweat and getting her flustered.

"You didn't get anything to drink. My mom's going to be upset with me for not using my manners if you are not sitting at that table with something in your mouth and with a glass of some kind of liquid in front of you. I'm gonna pick for you if you don't tell me."

That wasn't exactly using her manners, but sometimes life was more effective when she shucked the manners and opted for straight talk.

He chuckled. Yeah, he'd noticed she'd blown right by the manners and was aiming for results.

"If you have sweet tea, I'll take a glass of that. And whatever you put down in front of me, I'll have some of it in my mouth when your mom walks in the door."

She laughed, some of her tension and nervousness easing, as laughter always seemed to accomplish. "Wow. That was easy. I must be scary."

"Why do you assume that you're scary? Maybe I'm just nice."

"If I had to say, I would say I'm scary and you're nice."

He grunted.

She didn't have any homemade goodies to set in front of him, but she did find a half-empty package of Oreos in the cupboard, so she gave him some of those, although she couldn't imagine they paired well with the sweet tea. "Sorry. That's all I have. But if you give me a little warning as to when you're stopping by next time, I'll try to have something better."

"This is fine." He took a drink of his tea. "Thanks." There was a pause, as though he was checking his words to make sure they were proper. "What do you plan on doing while you're here in town?"

She stopped with her hand on the refrigerator door, her back to him. Then gave a mental shrug. There was no reason why she shouldn't tell him. She didn't know why she was so reluctant to talk about herself. Except she had a lot of things in her past that she wasn't exactly proud of.

She opened the door and set the tea down. She closed it and turned around before speaking. "I'm a farrier. If I'm staying here, depending on my mom's health, I'll be looking for work and for new clients, if you know anybody who needs one. If not, I'll be available this week anyway."

His eyebrows went up, and he nodded while his eyes skimmed over her. Not in a creepy way, but in a way she was used to when people found out she shod horses for a living. It was a job that required strength, and her muscles weren't bulky.

But to his credit, he didn't ask the question a lot of people, both men and women, asked when they found out what she did for a living—are you strong enough to handle that? Like somehow she managed to train to be a farrier for eighteen months and hadn't figured out until it was too late that she wasn't strong enough? The question didn't even make sense.

"I'll talk to Wilder Stryker. He raises some high-dollar horses, and he's got everything down to a science. I'm sure he has a farrier, but he might be looking for a backup."

That made her pause with her hand on the back of the chair that she'd been about to pull out and sit down on. "Really?" He hadn't asked for references or asked her if she was capable of doing the job; he just said he'd pass her name on. Just like that. "I really appreciate it. Sounds like that would be a good guy to get in with."

"Yeah. He would. An honest man and one who would treat you right. He pays his bills on time. You wouldn't have to worry about getting your money."

She almost snorted. Spoken like a farmer. In some circles, there were definitely people who thought it was low class to talk about finances. With farming, it was pretty much an everyday way of life.

"That's good to know." She slid the chair back and plopped down in it. "I haven't had too many people that have given me any problems paying." Farmers didn't typically have a lot of money, but in her experience, most of them paid their bills and didn't spend money they didn't have.

"I know a couple of other guys too. How far are you willing to travel?"

She lifted her shoulder. She hadn't thought about it, since she hadn't really been planning on staying. But with her mom the way she was, her mind had slowly been coming to terms with the fact that this could be permanent. At least for a while.

"As far as I need to right now while I'm building a client list. Eventually, it would be nice to not travel, say, more than an hour." She lowered her voice, because although she hadn't heard her mom come down the stairs, she didn't want her mom to know how...scared...she was at her condition. "I think Mom's going to need a lot of care. I wasn't expecting her to be this bad."

Again, Deacon's eyes seemed to hold compassion, understanding, and an astuteness she wasn't used to.

He tapped a finger on the table. "I know she sees her doctor regularly, but you might want to schedule an appointment. It does seem like she's gone rapidly downhill in the last two months. When I visit, she talks about having good days and bad days, but it always seems to be a bad day when I'm here."

"Okay. Good idea." She could talk to the doctor and see what he said. Her mom might talk about good days, but maybe she hadn't been having any.

The steps creaked, and she slid her chair back, intending to go see if her mom needed help. Deacon picked up one of the Oreos that she'd set in front of him and held it up.

Her eyes met his, and they shared a grin, remembering his promise and smiling because he was keeping it.

Like she would expect anything else from Deacon.

Deacon had totally put her at ease, which she would have said would be impossible for him to do. She had things to straighten up with him, somehow, but she almost forgot that when she was around him, because he was so...nice.

But more than that. Nice in a rugged and attractive way, but she could still feel the compassion practically ooze off him. That was where the guilt tripped her again, because he was born to be a pastor. And she'd messed that up.

Chapter 3

"Remember how I told you that Lynette was complaining about her back hurting, and how she was just tired?" Pastor Wyatt, or Gus, as Deacon called him when they were alone, arranged the already neat stack of new baptism Bibles on the desk in his office.

Deacon nodded, his ankle resting on his knee and his body slouched back in his chair. When Gus had first come and Deacon had started helping him, being in the office had bothered him, because he couldn't help thinking that it might have been his. It had taken him a little while to come to terms with the fact that God had a different plan for his life. Now, it was like a second home, and he loved Gus with all his heart.

"Her appointment was yesterday." There was a brief pause, as though Gus were trying to figure out how to say the next sentence. Finally, he just spit it out. "The doctor suspects cancer." The other man's eyes started tearing up, and he took his glasses off, wiping them with the end of his tie. He spoke with his face down, watching the material run over the glass. "They made us an appointment for the specialist next Wednesday. I don't know if I'll make it back in time for the prayer meeting. I was hoping you would do it for me, and I won't have to worry about it."

"You know I will." Deacon didn't even hesitate. Of all the things he had to do, preaching was probably the one where he felt least qualified. He'd taken all the classes, but he just hadn't stood in front of people enough to be totally comfortable. He could do it, though. The Wednesday night prayer meeting was more like teaching than preaching anyway.

"What kind of cancer?" He didn't want to pry or prod, but people were going to be asking, and he was curious himself. Lynette seemed indestructible.

"They're saying they're not sure but hinting that it might be some kind of bone marrow cancer. They think it will be curable, but they're sending us to a specialist, and fast. That makes me a little nervous."

Deacon shook his foot and tapped his fingers on his knee. It made him nervous too. Seemed like if they thought it wasn't bad and was curable, they wouldn't have gotten an appointment in less than five days.

"Maybe when you're visiting today, you can see if Mrs. Dixon's having a good day. I know she's been struggling lately, but she was always my go-to when I needed some help." Pastor put his elbow on his desk and dropped his head in his hand, like he just couldn't hold it up any longer. He seemed to gather himself enough to raise his eyes. "She's been Lynette's right hand for years. It's been so hard with her down and out most of the time. Anyway, if she could take over junior church for Lynette, that would be great."

Pastor was rambling just a little, but Deacon understood why. He'd be rambling too, if his wife had just been given a diagnosis of possible cancer.

It would turn one's world upside down; that was for sure.

Pastor also wasn't thinking straight. There was no way Mrs. Dixon was going to be able to teach junior church. She might be able to do a Sunday school class, especially of older elementary children or teens, where there wasn't too much physical work involved, since there wasn't anything wrong with her mind. It was her motor function that was affected.

That, and she was tired a lot.

But he didn't bother Pastor with that detail. "I'll talk to her about it. I'll make sure everything is covered for Wednesday."

He wasn't sure who else he could ask. Everyone who could do something was already doing it. He ran over a list of people in his mind. Surely there was someone.

He'd figure something out.

"I appreciate it." Pastor put his glasses back on his nose, and some of the worry lines on his face eased. "I really do appreciate having someone I can trust and depend on to take care of things when I can't be here. I don't know what all this is going to entail, but how willing are you to step up even more?"

Deacon studied the older man.

Pastor wasn't older by much, but Deacon sometimes felt like a wet-behind-the-ears kid beside him. He supposed it was just typical insecurities.

Everyone felt them, but he didn't know how many times over the years he'd been grateful that God hadn't opened the door to the pastorate and had brought Tinsley into his life instead. Probably just as many as he'd resented the fact that God hadn't opened the door and brought Tinsley into his life instead.

Not that he resented Tinsley, because he didn't. It was simply sometimes he was happy with the way things worked out, and sometimes he wondered, what if...

They talked more about logistics and things that could happen and their schedule for Sunday services before Deacon got up to go get started on his weekly afternoon visiting.

Mrs. Dixon was almost always his first stop, since she was in town not far from the church.

As Deacon left the church, he had to admit he was kind of excited to see Blair again. He'd run into her a couple of times in town, just to wave hi.

With her past and reputation, he probably shouldn't be thinking about her the way he was. He'd been in college when she'd gone to prison, and he wasn't sure exactly what she'd gone for. He could ask his parents or any of his brothers, but for some reason, he hadn't. He wasn't sure exactly why. Maybe he didn't want to seem too interested. They wouldn't think it was any more appropriate than he did.

It certainly wasn't something he could ask in polite conversation elsewhere. He wouldn't dream of asking Mrs. Dixon or Blair herself.

Blair seemed personable and nice—the way he'd remembered her from high school. Maybe she was a little bit snottier back then, but life had a way of humbling one. A prison sentence, probably even more.

He'd also heard she'd been pregnant at the time, but since he'd been in college, he'd gotten his information in bits and pieces, and he assumed, since she didn't have a child with her, that she'd done what most women in that situation would have done and "taken care" of it.

The thought clinched his stomach a little, both at the idea of a baby dying and at the idea of a mother so desperate she would kill her own child. Neither one of those two thoughts sat well with him.

He parked his truck in front of Mrs. Dixon's house and got out. He'd almost brought Tinsley with him today—he often did in the summer—but she'd just gotten out of school for the year, and she wanted to play with her cousins.

She and RaeAnne had gotten pretty close since Chandler and Ivory had gotten engaged. Their wedding was coming up in a little over a month, and Chandler had asked Deacon to officiate.

It'd taken five years for the bit of scandal to die down and for him to have the heart to try again, but he had been ordained about the time Tinsley went to kindergarten. He probably could go find another church, but he loved Cowboy Crossing and the people here, and he loved his ranch too. He'd work for free doing what he felt was God's work. Work that he loved.

He held a hand up and took a breath before he knocked on the door. Despite his curiosity about Blair, that was all it could be. Curiosity. If he had a hope and prayer of ever being a pastor, he would take that opportunity. She wouldn't be interested in being a pastor's wife.

He and Inez had decided to go out without the children the Saturday after next. They'd decided maybe it would be easier if they weren't so distracted watching their kids.

The elephant in his stomach stomped around.

Funny, because he wasn't the slightest bit nervous about seeing Inez a week from Saturday. A real date didn't make him nearly as nervous as he was about even knocking on Mrs. Dixon's door knowing that Blair might answer it.

Human emotions were so fickle and illogical.

Lord, why did you make us like this?

He was just about to knock again when the door opened and the scent of cinnamon and sugar and the stench of something burning mixed together to form a putrid mass that hit him not quite as hard as a bowling ball but enough to make him take a step back.

"Deacon. Right on time," Blair said, a spatula in one hand and an oven mitt on her other. She also had flour on one cheek and a little bit of what looked like batter on one lip.

"You were eating the evidence."

Her eyes widened, and immediately her tongue came out, licking her lips. She caught the spot and grinned. "Busted."

Her eyes, which had been sparkling, dimmed a little, and he thought maybe she was thinking of a prison reference. He supposed he should be too. But he wasn't thinking prison when he looked at her lips and saw her tongue.

He'd long since pulled his eyes away and held his Bible in front of him almost like a shield.

"I was expecting you. And I was hoping that I could use my manners today, instead of offering stale store-bought cookies, but..." She sighed deeply, long-suffering. "I did not somehow morph into a magically wonderful baker since last time I tried to bake something. That was about ten years ago."

He laughed. "These things usually take practice."

"Well, the videos on YouTube make it look easy."

He lifted his brows. "That's pretty impressive. You were watching a video, following it, and still managed to make things smell that bad?"

Her brows lifted. "Looks like I'm not the only one that's not using my manners."

"Yeah, but my mother's not here to yell at me." He said that kind of low, so Mrs. Dixon, who was coming down the stairs, leaning heavily on the banister, couldn't hear him.

He smirked at Blair. Odd, since he didn't usually smirk, but he had to when he saw her widened eyes.

She whirled around. He stepped back to avoid being whacked by the spatula

"Deacon!" Mrs. Dixon said. "I thought that might be you. You're as dependable as clockwork." She took another step, carefully.

Deacon made a note to ask Blair if it were possible to move her to a room downstairs. She looked like she could fall down the steps at any minute.

Normally, he might wait to be invited in, which Blair had never done, but he stepped in, closing the door behind him, and strode over, walking up the last five steps and offering a hand, which Mrs. Dixon accepted.

"It's funny," she said, putting her hand in his with a relieved sigh. "When you get older, you get a lot more afraid of falling down."

"That's normal. When you get older, you can get hurt a lot worse from a fall." He had visited enough elderly folks to know that was entirely true.

Blair looked at him oddly, maybe thinking for the first time that her mother might be old. She wasn't, necessarily, but MS had a way of aging a person.

Mrs. Dixon paused three steps from the top. She sniffed, then looked at her daughter. "What is that smell?"

Blair's lips flattened, but she also seemed to have a bit of a twinkle in her eye. "Mom, if you are just now smelling that, I think your nose might be plugged."

Mrs. Dixon sniffed. Again. "You know, I thought I might be catching a little cold."

"I think that smell might be the refreshments that Blair made for us today." Deacon couldn't help the lopsided grin that tilted half of his face up. It felt like a little teasing, and he enjoyed the red in her cheeks and the flash of her eyes.

"If you want me to serve it to you, I can."

"That's what you made it for, isn't it?"

"I didn't think I was going to make you eat something that was burnt black a full inch from the bottom of the pan and you have to use a chisel and a hacksaw to get out."

"That bad?"

She nodded. "I was on the phone with a man I found online, talking about a farrier job." She lifted a hand. "I totally forgot about the stuff in the oven. Makes me mad too, because I think that it actually would have tasted good for once. I know I put sugar and not salt in it, anyway."

Mrs. Dixon chuckled a little at that, and Deacon was thankful to hear that she seemed happy, despite her increased physical limitation.

"Where's Tinsley?" Mrs. Dixon asked as her foot touched down on the floor. Solid footing at last.

If Deacon hadn't been looking at Blair, thinking about how much he enjoyed teasing her, he might not have noticed the widening of her eyes or the whitening of her knuckles as she held the spatula in her hand.

"I'm going to run into the kitchen and see if there's anything there that's salvageable."

She strode down the hall without looking back. Odd behavior. He would have no idea why, except possibly the idea of Tinsley reminded her of the baby that she'd killed. He'd counselled a few ladies who had that guilt eating at them decades later.

Maybe that wasn't it. It was just an assumption. He supposed he should find out for sure, because assumptions weren't nice and were often wrong.

"She's with my mom. She and RaeAnne have gotten close, and I think Zane's boys were over as well. Along with Marlowe and Clark's kids. My poor mom, although she loves it."

Mrs. Dixon's hands held tightly to his arm as they shuffled down the hall. "I bet she loves it. She doesn't look like a hefty woman, but she raised you boys just fine, and she seemed to enjoy doing it. I just had one child, and sometimes I feel like God gave me too much."

"I know my mom had her moments," Deacon said. They had reached the doorway to the kitchen, and he held Mrs. Dixon's chair out while she fell heavily into it.

"How are things going at church?" Mrs. Dixon asked, a little out of breath.

Deacon stood at the end of the table, aware of Blair's movements behind him, feeling her presence more strongly than a physical touch. "Miss Lynette is going to the doctor's on Wednesday, and Pastor needs someone to teach junior church. He mentioned you, and I promised to say something, but I know you've been having some bad days lately. No hard feelings if you can't."

Mrs. Dixon sighed a heavy, hard, depressing sigh.

Deacon looked at her, and there was a little corner of his brain that said, *Why, God? Why are You making her do this?*

But he knew. He truly did know, and he understood. Hardships made a person better. Going through something like this, the struggle, would give a person character. Partly because of the struggle, and partly because it made them lean more heavily on the Lord. Made them think more about the next world than the world they were in, realizing that making themselves happy in the here and now wasn't the end goal of life.

Yeah, the struggle was good for them, but it was so hard to watch.

Chapter 4

Blair had practiced this coffee cake earlier in the week, and it had turned out fine. Well, mostly fine. It was a little soggy in the middle, but it wasn't like Deacon was going to get to the middle today.

She tried to focus on the cake and ignore the pinch of her heart as he walked into the kitchen, standing and talking to her mom for a minute before he walked around the kitchen table and sat across from her. He was just the same way he was the last time, and his movements were just as sure, almost graceful.

The way she'd done it had been wrong, but she'd picked the right man for her daughter.

Opening the cupboard door, she took the same package of chocolate sandwich cookies out that she'd served him last week and set them on the table. "I'm sorry. At least you know I tried."

Her mother gave her a look, one that she was familiar with growing up. One that said she was disappointed in her daughter. Blair had seen that look a billion times. She'd been one big disappointment to her mother her whole life.

Her mom didn't mean her to take it that way. Really. She just didn't understand why Blair wasn't like her—little Susie homemaker, an upstanding citizen in their tiny town, and president of every committee at church. The local do-gooder.

She'd been more like the local rebel, although she'd been popular in high school, and her mom had seemed proud when she'd worn the homecoming crown.

She wouldn't have been proud of what she'd done later that night. Thankfully, her mom probably didn't even know.

Blair's eyes skittered to Deacon. He wouldn't know either. He didn't run with her crowd, and he'd been home in bed in order to get up early to go do some kind of farming thing the next day.

"Mom, would you like some water with your pills?" she asked.

"Yes, please." Her mother moved her hands across the top of the table and clasped them together. Probably to make it less obvious that she couldn't stop them from shaking.

Not for the first time since she'd been home, fear pushed up her backbone.

They had a doctor's appointment in two weeks. Hopefully she'd know more then. In the meantime, she figured she might as well plan on staying right here. She needed to go back and clean out the apartment she had in Francisville in northwest Missouri. Some time.

She had enough of her things for now, but she didn't want to have to keep paying rent on it. Thankfully, there was no lease.

"Would you like sweet tea again?" she asked Deacon, forcing herself to meet his eyes. She wouldn't let herself take the coward's way out.

She wanted to do something about him as well.

"I think milk would go better with these," he said. "If it's not too much trouble."

She rolled her eyes. "It's not too much trouble. And you're right. Milk probably is much better."

She opened the refrigerator door, trying to stop the silly smile that hovered over her mouth. They were talking about cookies and milk. Mundane. And yet her heart was fluttering and she couldn't keep from smiling.

She'd get a handle on it. He was one man who was totally off-limits for her. Even if she didn't have the sticky situation about her daughter, he wanted to be a preacher. He didn't want to have a woman with a prison record as his wife. And he'd want a wife, not a fling.

She'd never really been a wife kinda girl.

She set the milk down in front of him and then gave her mother her noon pills along with a glass of water.

Figuring that she'd go somewhere else and give them a little privacy, she was startled when Deacon spoke. "Aren't you going to sit down with us?"

Her mom had been talking about the neighbors who used to live beside them and the years when her mom had taught Deacon in Sunday school. Blair hadn't really thought she'd be a part of that conversation. She'd gone to Sunday school, but she hadn't been in Deacon's class, and her mom had dragged her there kicking and screaming. She'd quit as soon as she was allowed, which was when she moved out of the house.

But Deacon pulled her in ways she couldn't even explain. She found herself pulling a chair out and sitting down.

Her mom's hands trembled as she picked up the pills Blair had set beside her water. "I really wish I could do junior church. There's a part of me that just loves to help and be needed, but I don't know if I'll be having a good day or a bad day, and I hate to commit."

It would be easier to hire a caregiver. Blair's heart cringed in her chest. After everything she'd put her mother through, it didn't seem right to give her care over to someone else, too.

But it was so hard to see her mom like this. She hadn't had a single "good" day since Blair had come back. It was almost a guarantee that next Wednesday wouldn't be good.

"What do you say to that, Blair?"

"Huh?" She blinked her eyes and looked at Deacon. Apparently, he'd said something to her. She'd thought she was just gonna sit and listen to their conversation. She hadn't planned on participating and, hence, paying attention.

"I said you could teach the kids' club on Wednesday night if your mom isn't having a good day."

She shook her head even before the word came out of her mouth. "No."

But she happened to look over at her mom and saw that disappointed look again. The one that she'd received all through her teenage years. The one that she could never quite get turned into a smile of approval.

"I'll pay you double what the regular teacher makes." Deacon didn't even crack a smile.

She knew that for the baloney it was. Then she grinned. "I might not be the best at math, but I know exactly what double of zero is. I'm pretty sure that since I went to Sunday school, the pay hasn't gone up."

Deacon paused with a cookie hovering in front of his mouth. "I think it's gotten worse."

She lifted her brows at that. "It can't get worse than zero."

"How do you know we're not going to charge you for the privilege of teaching?"

"Okay. You win. It does get worse than zero." She giggled. She hadn't giggled since probably kindergarten or earlier.

She happened to see, as she was reaching for a cookie, that her mom's look of disapproval, while it maybe hadn't turned into complete approval, had changed some. That made her smile grow even bigger.

Maybe her mom was sick, and maybe she wasn't going to get better, but maybe Blair could finally, after all the years of heartache, make her mom smile.

How hard it must have been for the Sunday school teacher and the upstanding woman in the community to face her friends and neighbors knowing her daughter was in prison.

That familiar tight ball of heat pressed against her heart. It made swallowing difficult.

"I think she's thinking about it, Mrs. Dixon," Deacon said softly.

She wanted to toss her head and say "in your dreams." No, maybe only part of her wanted to do that. A bigger part of her was on board when she turned her head to Deacon.

"Okay. I'll do it."

His face wreathed into a full-on grin, and her heart stopped. Man, he was way too handsome to be a preacher. Preachers shouldn't make her catch her breath and tempt her to want to move closer.

She tore her eyes away and met her mother's gaze, proud and happy and smiling.

Yeah. She had no idea how to teach kids' club. Her past... Her eyes got wide. Deacon must not know. She seemed to recall he was in Bible college when that all went down.

Of course, she'd met with him once, just because he was the only one she knew whom she could talk to and wouldn't judge her, but he hadn't said anything she didn't already know and she was too stupid to take good advice.

But he'd gone back to school and might not have heard what had happened.

It was kind of impossible to think for one second he hadn't, but...if he knew...if he knew about Tinsley, this whole conversation wouldn't be happening. He wouldn't be sitting at the table with her.

"Cold feet already? Isn't that supposed to happen a little closer to the date? You have six days." His words were light and easy, but his expression had darkened into concern.

"You don't know," she whispered, horrified and embarrassed. More horrified and embarrassed than she'd been even when she had been sentenced in the courtroom and hauled away in handcuffs. Her wide eyes went to her mom, and she gripped her mother's hand. "He doesn't know."

She had to be an adult about this. She couldn't act like an underaged teenager who had just gotten caught with a can of beer. She straightened her shoulders and loosened her fingers on her mother's wrinkled hand.

Her mother tightened her grip, so she didn't pull her fingers completely away but faced Deacon.

"I was in prison. I'm hardly church teacher material."

He stared at her. Long enough for it to be uncomfortable for her, and she wanted to squirm. She did move her feet under the table, but she kept her butt still and met his eyes second by second by uncomfortable second. She wouldn't back down. It was her past, and she would own up to it.

"You think, living in this small town my whole life, I didn't know that?" he finally asked, softly and kind of incredulously.

"Churches must be a lot more desperate for teachers than they were when I was growing up. You're really scraping the bottom of the barrel with me."

"That's ridiculous." He shook his head. "I think you'll do a really great job. You can tell the kids from personal experience what could happen if they don't do what their parents tell them to. You have great personal experience to draw from."

She dropped her eyes to her hands, but they flicked back to his. Somehow, those words coming from him didn't sound trite. It also didn't sound like he was judging her.

"You know," he said, "some people have really great testimonies about how they were saved from deep sin. They're dramatic, and people can relate to them because they see those people as people who understand." He held his hands up. "I don't have that. I've been a church boy my whole life."

"You say that like it's a bad thing."

"You know as well as I do that to some people it is."

She couldn't argue with that. To most people, anymore. Probably. She nodded.

"You can reach people that I can't." He lifted his brows in challenge. "Kids that I can't. Kids that Lynette can't. Because they can relate to you, where they just see me as a goody-goody."

Yeah. She had been one of those kids who would have seen him as a goody-goody back when they were younger. Although she'd always liked Deacon. He had been a goody-goody that hadn't seemed like a goody-goody at the time.

"Okay. But I've never taught anything before."

Her mother patted her hand. "You had teachers. Simply do what they did. It's not hard."

"And food. You gotta have..." Deacon's eyes slid to the burnt coffee cake in the pan still sitting on the counter. "Never mind. Maybe you should just bring chocolate milk."

She laughed. "Maybe I could find some doughnuts somewhere."

"The kids like these." Her mother pointed at the chocolate sandwich cookies on the table.

She could do that. It wasn't hard to go to the grocery store and pick up a package. It wouldn't require her to bake for the third time since she'd returned to Cowboy Crossing.

"Plus, your mom said she'd help you if she can." Deacon reached across the table and put his hand on top of her mother's other hand. Her mother turned her hand and gripped his fingers. It was odd to see, but it was almost like her mother drew strength from Deacon and his touch. Like there was something, not mystical or magical, but some kind of pure and spiritual strength.

Blair wasn't even touching him, and she felt it.

But watching her mother was enough to make Blair wish that there was a reason for her to hold Deacon's hand. Not for the attraction, although it might be partly, but because there was so much honor and integrity in him it couldn't help but rub off. So much confidence and assurance in God the Father that it almost communicated through his actions.

"I will, honey," her mom said. "If I can," she added in a softer, less certain note.

Chapter 5

Deacon tapped his notes on the table, straightening the edges so they were all in an organized pile.

Pastor Wyatt typically had his notes on an iPad which he used from the pulpit, but Deacon felt better with the paper in his hand. He'd always been a hands-on kind of guy. And having his Bible in one hand and his notes in the other gave him comfort that electronic devices just couldn't emulate.

He had two hours until church. He'd deliberately planned that way, because he wanted to be here early and be prepared. Now, he walked into the sanctuary, intending to kneel at every seat and pray over it.

He hadn't made it out of the back row when his phone buzzed. Hoping it wasn't some kind of emergency, he saw it was Pastor Wyatt before he swiped.

"Hello?"

"Deacon. They did some blood work here in the office on Lynette, and they want to send her directly out to St. Louis and admit her at the hospital there. It's a little more serious than what they were thinking."

Deacon was already on his knees. His stomach seemed to land there too. His entire body felt hot then cold. He gripped the phone tighter. "How serious?"

He knew it was really unusual for Lynette to be tired, and she'd actually even missed two church services. Then this news. It didn't sound good.

"They're not really telling us. They just say they want to get more tests in St. Louis."

"How's Lynette?" She'd complained about some pain. She also seemed like she was so in control, and this definitely wasn't something she could control.

"She's doing really well. I know she's organized and runs things efficiently, and though this is outside what she's comfortable with, she's also deeply spiritual. She has one hand holding mine and one hand holding onto God's. She's as fine as anyone I've ever seen in this situation."

Deacon blew out a breath. Wow. He didn't think he'd be quite that calm with a serious diagnosis like this. Although there was more anxiety in Pastor Wyatt's voice than he had ever heard before.

It was a real blessing that Lynette was calm.

"That's good," he finally said. What else was there to say?

"Yes. But what I was really calling about was I don't know how long they're going to be keeping us. They don't know either. They said something about starting treatments immediately if certain tests come back in certain ways..." His voice trailed off, and Deacon could almost see him pacing back and forth in a sterile waiting room somewhere, shoving a hand through his hair and scared to death about his wife.

"It's okay. All your information is probably running together."

"Yes. I've made a lot of hospital visits, but they're using words I've never heard before, and I don't like the survival rate they gave us. Please don't say anything along those lines to the congregation tonight."

"No. Of course. No."

"So that's one of the reasons I called. To give you an update that you can give to our church family. But also, if they start treatments, they said it would be several days, and I'm not sure I'll make it home to preach on Sunday. I can call someone else if you can't do it."

"You don't have to do that. I've got it covered as long as you're away."

There was a pause, like Pastor was collecting himself. His voice was scratchy when he said, "I knew you would. Thank you."

They spoke for a few more short sentences. Deacon made sure that their eight children were being taken care of and that Lynette had everything she needed from home, and they ended the call. Obviously, Gus wanted to get back to his wife.

Deacon's mind raced. Not only would he be covering for Gus, but he would need to find someone to cover for Lynette's Sunday school class. He'd also been going to counsel a teen girl tomorrow afternoon, and usually Lynette sat in the counseling sessions with him. He'd either have to cancel or call...

Without his permission, Blair's face came into his mind. He couldn't seem to stop thinking about her. He'd been looking forward to seeing her tonight. Excited. He should be focusing on his message, and he was, but she'd creep into the corners of his mind at the oddest times.

He couldn't think about her. He shouldn't think about her. Funny, because she was all he wanted to think about. He'd even forgotten about his date with Inez on Saturday night. Funny how he dreaded that, and yet just the idea of seeing Blair at church had him looking around to see if she might have arrived yet. He was foolish.

He checked his phone. Still plenty of time to finish praying before his mom showed up with Tinsley. Seemed like Tinsley was spending more time with his mom than she was with him lately. The newness of being out of school and playing with her cousins would probably wear off, but he couldn't blame her. He had a blast with his brothers playing on the farm growing up. His parents didn't live in the house that they lived in now, but there'd been a creek and a barn, and his brothers and he had spent hours playing hide-and-seek and splashing, swimming, and fishing in the creek.

With all the pressure of the evening, just thinking about the happy memories from his childhood pushed it away, and in its place came a longing, unlike anything he'd ever felt before. A longing for a home and family of his own. A mother for Tinsley and the happy sounds of children as they moved through their life. Sweet looks from his wife and a baby to snuggle in his arms. Boys to be an example for and blessed communion around God's word.

Inez would be the perfect woman to have that with, but it wasn't her face that he saw in his mind's eye.

A HALF AN HOUR BEFORE church was to start, Blair walked through the door. Deacon was carrying the toilet bowl cleaner out of the men's restroom after cleaning the restroom and scrubbing the toilets. He stopped in the doorway and watched her walk in.

That crazy part of him that wanted to do nothing but stand and watch her got a hold of him.

He was surprised that she wore a skirt, and it flowed around her legs, cute and flirty, and suited the personality that she had when she was a teenager, but he wasn't sure about now. She'd changed. They'd all changed from when they were teens. He'd like to see her smiling and having fun again, without that big cloud of guilt and regret that seemed to sit squarely on her back most of the time.

Normally her walk was confident, even tough, but tonight it was much less sure. She didn't quite tiptoe through the door, but she was definitely out of her element, and he appreciated the fact that she was even there.

Her face brightened when she saw him, and he lifted the toilet bowl cleaner in a wave, which made her anxious lines dissolve into a smile.

"I thought you were the preacher for tonight? Doesn't that put you a little above scrubbing the toilets?"

"I'm pretty sure that puts me directly at scrubbing the toilets," he said as he walked toward the supply closet to put the cleaning equipment away. "Actually, I always scrub the toilets before church."

"I've never known a man who scrubbed toilets before. At least not without getting paid for it."

"Oh, I'm getting paid for it."

"I thought you said your job was gratis?"

"It is. Not for money anyway. God's keeping track, and I know He's good for it."

She shook her head a little, but her lips were still pulled back so he thought she might find his heavenly humor, if not hilarious, at least laughable.

He closed the closet door and walked over to her. "Did your mom give you some lesson books?" he asked, pointing to the manuals she had clutched in her arms, holding them in front of her chest like they would somehow protect her. He couldn't help teasing her. "I'm pretty sure they won't stop a bullet."

Her brows drew together before she grinned. Her body seemed to loosen a little like her laughter made her realize how tense she was.

"No, these have some game ideas in them, and some stories in case I blow through whatever the actual lesson is supposed to be. Basically, these are my backup in case I have to kill time because the preacher runs over tonight."

"I could probably put in a good word for you and see if he could stop on time or maybe even five minutes early."

"Well, go ahead and do that. Ten minutes early wouldn't be too much."

"You're going to be just fine, you know, Blair. You're going to be good at this. I'd almost bet money on it."

"I hardly think you're the betting kind."

Deacon dropped his eyes. It hadn't been that long ago that he actually had bet quite a large sum of money. It hadn't all been his. His brothers, except for Chandler, had all gotten together along with his parents and contributed enough for him to pick a person to buy Chandler at auction. It was kind of like a family intervention, only way down on the sly, and his brother still didn't know about it. Deacon had given half the money to Ivory, taking a chance that the bidding wouldn't go any higher. Then, he'd made a major bet on Chandler sticking it out with the rest.

He'd won that bet, doubled his money, and his family had donated it all to the tornado victims that the auction was benefiting.

It hadn't turned him into a betting man, but it had definitely been a step into a gray area that he didn't care to repeat.

"Do you have a gambling problem?" Blair asked softly, her question underscored with concern and maybe a little bit of amazement.

It was the concern that warmed his soul.

"No." That was the truth.

"You just looked kinda funny there for a minute." Her eyes narrowed. "You probably wouldn't tell me if you did have a problem."

"I wouldn't want to," he said honestly. "But I don't."

"There was something..." She trailed off, inviting him to answer without asking an outright question.

"Maybe we can talk about it sometime. But I promise it's not a gambling addiction." It was too complicated to get into now, and he wasn't going to say he just recently made a large money bet without explaining it.

"Are you telling me the preacher has some skeletons in his closet?" She tilted her head and smiled just a little. If he didn't know better, he'd think she was flirting with him.

He kept his expression serious, unwilling to give in to the idea that she might be being more than friendly. It was a dangerous path for him to go down. With the attraction he already felt toward her, he could lose his heart to this woman if he wasn't careful.

She wouldn't feel a thing.

"I think we all have things we struggle with," he finally said, when it looked like she'd wait all night for him to speak.

"I'll take you up on your suggestion then. We'll go talk about it. How about Saturday night? We can call it a date." She said the last with a goofy look, probably so he didn't think that she actually meant a date date. Although Saturday night...it could mean date date.

Actually, it did mean a date for him. Just not with Blair.

"I can't do it Saturday night. And not Sunday either, because Pastor Wyatt called just an hour or so ago and asked me to take care of the services on Sunday because the doctors are sending his wife to St. Louis."

Her face had gone through several expressions while he was talking, and he was pretty sure she was gonna press him about why he couldn't do anything with her on Saturday night. He didn't want to admit he was already going on a date with someone else, because he didn't want to do that without explaining that it didn't mean anything and about Lynette setting them up and it was too complicated to hash out now.

"Is it that bad?" Her voice was softer and full of concern.

It took him a minute to remember they were talking about Lynette. "Sounds like it might be. But they don't know for sure, so there's no point in jumping to conclusions. They're gonna do more testing, and I won't say anything alarming to the congregation tonight." Implied in that statement was that he had told her more than he was going to tell them, which kind of made her special. Maybe she was. To him.

She nodded, the expression on her face saying she understood that she shouldn't say anything to anyone.

"That leaves me in a little bit of a bind for tomorrow, though." He hadn't really planned on saying that, but the words started coming out, and he liked the idea as it was turning in his mind. "Normally Lynette sits with me when I counsel women."

"Why?" She sounded truly perplexed.

He stared hard at her for a minute, then decided to just be honest. "It's for my protection. I know two men who are serving prison terms right now because they were counseling underage teenage girls, and they ended up being inappropriate. I also know another man who lost his job because he was counseling a teenager who lied about him. They were alone in his office together, and it was her word against his. The accusations were bad enough that the church wasn't taking any chances, and he was fired. A decade later, the girl admitted she lied.

"Seems I can learn a lot from the mistakes of others. So I don't counsel anyone of the opposite sex unless there is someone else there. Usually when I'm counseling a woman, I try to have a woman with me. Just to make it less awkward." His eyes were serious, and she had met his gaze the whole time. Understanding dawned and then reluctant admiration. He liked that look.

"You're doing a lot of favors for me," he said, holding up his hand. "But I think I might be able to do you a good turn. I called Wilder Stryker about a farrier job at his ranch, and I've got a message on my phone from him.

"I heard, just this afternoon, from Tracy, a nurse at the ER who starts the prayer chain, that his regular farrier had a bad fall from a horse and had a broken arm and three broken ribs. I'm guessing the call from Wilder is asking about the farrier that I had mentioned to him last time we spoke." He raised his brows.

Her mouth had formed an "O," but by the time he was done, the corners of it tilted up. "I remember Wilder, but now he has the high-dollar racehorses?"

"Yup. He does a lot of horse training. Not just racehorses, but he also does Western and dressage. He's into horses in a big way. The position probably wouldn't be full-time, but it would be a great start."

"I don't know if I could do full-time anyway. Someone has to take care of Mom. I left her alone tonight, but with the promise that she wouldn't try to go to bed without me. She's in the living room watching TV."

"She should be fine. But if you ever have any problems, you know you can call me."

"Yes. I don't have your number, but I'm sure Mom does."

He didn't typically give his number out directly; that felt a little too personal. But he hadn't really been typical with Blair. He pulled his phone out. "What's your number, I'll send you a text." He put the info in while she rattled off her number and then sent her a simple text of "hi."

"Thanks," she said as her phone dinged in her pocket. She pulled it out and swiped and clicked on her screen.

"Do you want me to take you back and show you where your room is?"

"If you wouldn't mind. Once you show me where it is, you can leave and get back to the other things that you need to do. I promise I'll be okay." She pushed her hair out of her face. "I know I look like I'm a wreck, but if I can handle three years in prison, I can handle a bunch of nine- and ten-year-olds."

Her words were brave, and she threw that prison sentence phrase out there like she was throwing up roadblocks between them. Which was just fine with him. He didn't want to hate her, but he didn't want to feel this annoying attraction either.

Especially because he'd been admiring her for coming in when she was obviously uncomfortable. For being willing to teach and fill a need. For caring for her mother and, if he'd figured correctly, feeling guilty for all the pain she'd put her through.

For someone like him, teaching kids' club was easy. For someone like Blair, it was a huge, scary step. He was accepted and beloved inside these walls. She was an outcast, and there were almost certainly people who would not want her there.

He admired her courage.

Leading her down the stairs, he took her to the classroom beyond the rec room. "We usually teach all the older elementary kids on Wednesday in this room. They'll all know to come in, so you can hang out here and work on your lesson. They'll arrive eventually."

She nodded as he kept explaining, and he tried to focus on what he knew about junior church. He often floated around during services, just making sure everything was okay, making sure no one was coming in who didn't belong. He had a pretty good idea of how things were run.

He ended by saying, "I'm sorry I won't be able to help you if you have any trouble, since I'll be leading the service. But I know that any one of my brothers will give you a hand. I'll make sure I say something before church starts. So they'll be expecting it in case you need them."

She took a deep breath, and her chin was up, but she shifted. He wasn't fooled. But he couldn't blame her for being nervous. He was nervous too. Maybe that would help her.

"You know, I don't teach in front of people very often; my work is mostly behind the scenes. I'm pretty nervous about tonight, too."

"Really?" She shifted her eyes down then back up. "I couldn't tell it to look at you. And you sound so calm."

"No, the elephants in my stomach are playing hopscotch, no doubt. But I do have a good feeling, because I know that the work is necessary and God wants it done. I know He'll help me with it."

She bit her lip. "I actually prayed about this before I left tonight. It feels like a big responsibility to be in charge of the spiritual welfare of the next generation of little Christians. Especially when I've been such a bad example myself."

Praying was a good idea. He'd done enough of it himself all day today. But he lifted his hand up, and it hovered over her shoulder. "Do you mind?"

He wasn't entirely convinced it was what she wanted, because there were lines between her brows, but she nodded.

He put his hand on her shoulder and said a short prayer of thankfulness and petition.

He dropped his hand immediately after the amen.

"Thank you," she whispered.

He hadn't been expecting that, and he nodded.

He didn't want to leave. On a normal night, he wouldn't have to. "If you don't mind, I'd better get back upstairs."

"No, of course. Thank you so much for your time."

He wanted to do his job, his duty, and do it well. But it was really hard to turn and walk away from her.

Chapter 6

You never said what time you need to meet tomorrow.

Blair's hand hovered over the send button before she hit it.

Her mom was in bed, and she was headed there herself. Class with the kids went pretty well, although her methods of teaching were maybe a little unconventional. They acted out the story instead of having her stand there and tell it. There might have been a little more noise and a lot more movement than usual, but the kids all seemed to have a good time, and she thought she might've done okay.

But she left without talking to Deacon again. He'd been caught up in conversation with several older ladies and older gentlemen, and she needed to hurry out and get back home to her mother.

Still, she'd be seeing him again since he'd asked her to sit with him during a counseling session tomorrow. He'd never given her a time.

Maybe he was already in bed. It was later than she would text or call her mom.

Her phone beeped; she held it up.

Sorry. Four p.m. Does that mean you can make it?

Yes. At the church?

Yes.

She was debating about whether to say good night or not when her phone beeped again with another text from him.

I get off work at twelve. I'll have Tinsley with me, but we could go see Wilder Stryker and talk to him about the farrier job if you'd like, since that's what his message was about, but I didn't get a chance to tell you.

I'd love that.

I'll pick you up after work.

If he'd said what his actual job was, she couldn't remember, and her mother had never talked about him outside his assistant pastor position.

With that said, a little flurry of guilt went through her, because if it weren't for her, his job might have been a full-time pastor.

Her mom had been one of his biggest supporters. When the baby had shown up on the day he was supposed to be ordained and he'd lost that opportunity, her mom had been extremely upset. Blair had heard about it over and over again for months.

But she'd also heard what a great father he was, and how good he was with the baby, and how Deacon had said that it was God's will for him to be a father at this point in his life.

Of course, her mom had made sure to tell her, two years ago, when Deacon had been ordained. Finally. Too late to get the church in Cowboy Crossing.

He'd never seemed to be interested in looking for a church somewhere else.

Okay, I'll be watching for you.

She didn't want to let him go. She wanted to keep chatting. Maybe she was just lonely, because she'd spent most of the time since she'd come to Cowboy Crossing taking care of her mother and catching up on the cleaning and other chores around the house. But even as she thought that, she knew it wasn't true. There was just something about Deacon. She didn't have to wonder though, because her phone dinged with another text.

Good night.

That took the decision from her, and she texted back.

Good night.

The next day, she was ready at twelve, and he was there at ten after.

She dressed with a little more care than usual, not just because she was going to see Deacon, but because he said he was bringing Tinsley.

But he was alone in his pickup when she opened the passenger door without waiting for him to get out.

"I thought you were bringing Tinsley?" she said before she got in.

"I'm sorry. I didn't think it through. My mom keeps her during the mornings while I work. Sometimes she hangs out at the feed store with Marlowe and some of her cousins, but not today."

Disappointment was sharp in her chest; she'd thought she was going to see her daughter. Not that she had any claim on her, and not that she would take any. Not after the way she'd left her off and rearranged Deacon's life. But no one could blame her for wanting to see her.

"I don't need to get all fancied up to go out and see Wilder. If it doesn't bother you, I'm just going to go in my work clothes."

His T-shirt was dusty, and so were his jeans. He wore work boots. A far cry from the way he was just last night at church. But it looked good. She liked the contradictions, although she would have guessed him for an office worker.

"You look fine to me." He looked more than fine, but she figured it probably was inappropriate for her to say so. She didn't want to ruin the trust he seemed to have placed in her.

"Is your mom going to be okay?"

She nodded. "She was sleeping when I left. It's only going to be a couple of hours, right?" She slammed the door closed. The window was already down, so she buckled her belt and hung her elbow over the side.

After waiting for her to buckle her seatbelt, he pulled out.

"I don't even think it will take that long, although Wilder might want to give you a tour of the facility, and he'll probably want to let you know what you're getting into and what he expects. His horses are pretty valuable."

"I'm surprised that he didn't ask for references or anything like that."

Deacon's fingers tightened on the steering wheel, and he shifted his eyes over to glance at her before he looked back at the road.

"What did that look mean?"

"It meant I gave my word that you're good."

"What do you mean by 'good'?" she asked, although his words had seemed to fill her chest, making it expand in a good, happy way.

"Dependable. Able to do your job well. Basically, a person he can trust a hundred-thousand-dollar horse to."

Blair had been around some expensive horses, and she was in the horse world enough to know what the price tag of some of them were. But she'd never actually shod one that was worth that much.

Her stomach tried to crawl out of her belly button, and she clinched her abs to try to get it settled down. Being nervous wasn't going to help anything. She should focus; she knew she was good at what she did. She worked hard at it.

Three years in prison had taught her that a job was a privilege she wouldn't take for granted again.

"How did you get into this anyway?"

It was nice of him not to say how did someone who was imprisoned end up being a horse farrier.

"They have programs for ex-prisoners. This was one of them, and I qualified. I figured I'd be a fool to not take advantage of it."

"So you did this after you got out of prison?"

"Yeah. I was on parole for a year and did most of it then. It was an eighteen-month program."

"Wow. It takes eighteen months?"

"You don't have to have a degree to do it." She laughed a little. "But I had no experience with horses and figured I needed to start somewhere. They were very thorough in the training, which is exactly what I needed."

He nodded like he understood. She thought maybe he did. "I admire that. Someone who works for what they want."

"I guess I can understand how a person who was imprisoned once could end up back there. When you get out, everything feels different and hard. It'd be easy to fall back into your old ways and go down the same road. But I swore that wouldn't be me."

He nodded. "So you've been doing this for a few years on your own then," he said, as he made the right to go out of town.

"Yes. It's not like you can get hired and work for a company. But it's surprising how much work you really have. I never had a problem staying busy. It is a little dicey at the beginning to scrounge up clients, but then it's just a matter of how long and how much you want to work."

"Nice. Sounds like being a pastor. There's always going to be a need. As long as there are suffering people, people getting married, and people dying."

Corn fields tall in tassel went by on either side as she stared out her window. "I never really thought about it that way, but you're there for the special occasions in people's lives."

"You wouldn't believe the birthday parties I get invited to. Anniversary parties."

She couldn't imagine wanting to have the preacher at her birthday party growing up.

He slanted a glance over at her, and she could read the humor on his face. "You don't have to say anything, I can see you're thinking you wouldn't want the preacher at your birthday party."

She laughed outright at that, her laughter being taken away by the wind blowing in the cab as he sped up outside of town. This beautiful summer day, marked by the clear blue sky and green and yellow fields surrounding them. A perfect day for a nice ride and a good conversation with a friend.

Only, Deacon wasn't her friend. He was just the pastor's assistant, and he was helping her because she was going to help him later this afternoon.

"So what do I have to do for this counseling thing?"

"Just sit there."

"Really? That's it?"

Deacon nodded. "A lot of times, I don't even do a lot of talking. People often know what they should do, they just don't want to do it. There's no point in me coming down on them like a ton of bricks. Sometimes they just need somebody to listen."

"You're definitely easy to talk to. I've been tempted to tell you things I've never told anyone." She laughed self-consciously. "Like that."

He lifted a hand from the steering wheel, proclaiming his innocence. "Sometimes you just keep your mouth shut, and people talk. But maybe, there is also less pressure since I'm not the actual pastor. Or maybe they just feel like they're not going to be judged."

"Yeah. That's hard. Small towns really do judge."

He tilted his head to the side. "There's nothing wrong with that, really. It's biblical. Being judged has a tendency to keep you from doing bad things. Because you know people are going to look down on you."

"I can't believe you just said it was okay to judge people."

"Wasn't me. It's Bible."

"But it also says to judge not. How can it be both?"

"People are always looking for contradictions, aren't they?"

"Just one contradiction nullifies the entire book."

"That's true. Maybe that's why we search for them. We want to make sure."

"Or we want to prove it wrong."

"True."

She shoved a piece of hair out of her face. "You never did explain the contradiction. I'm about to become an unbeliever right here."

He lifted a brow but didn't chuckle like she kinda thought he would. "We could spend hours talking about it. It's kind of a complicated concept."

"How about you just give me the one-line summary?"

He grunted. "That's what I thought. The kid can't take hard preaching."

"That's right. I have itching ears. Itch them."

He lifted a hand off the steering wheel and reached over like he was actually going to touch her ears. She laughed and batted it away, sure that he got the New Testament reference and was just being goofy. Actually, she was tempted to let him.

"I know you know what I meant."

"You're right." He took a deep breath and blew it out slowly, thinking. "We're not supposed to judge each other, meaning pass sentences of judgment on each other. That's God's job. But we are supposed to judge sin. We're not supposed to put up with it."

He put his turn signal on before turning into a dirt drive. The end of the drive had a mailbox with pretty flowers all around it.

"That was a little more than a sentence, but that's the best I can do. If you want to talk about it sometime though, I sure will."

"I would." She wouldn't turn down an opportunity to talk to Deacon. It was pretty obvious that he couldn't be shaken from what he believed, and she admired that. Maybe someday she'd have faith like that. Half of the time, she wondered if God was really real; the other half of the time, she was convinced He hated her. But when she was lucid, she could admit that most of the problems in her life had been brought on by her own stupidity.

"That's what I thought," he said, sounding sarcastic.

"No, actually, I was just thinking I really would."

The truck slowed to a crawl, and Blair wondered if it was because Deacon didn't want the ride to end, or maybe he still had something more to say.

He took a hand off the steering wheel and put it on his leg, almost like his palms were sweating.

"Maybe Sunday afternoon, you'd like to take a picnic to the creek with Tinsley and me?"

His words came out low. It was a good thing they weren't going very fast, because the wind would have taken them away easily.

It was hard to imagine a man like Deacon being nervous, but she almost thought that maybe that was what it was. "You turned me down for Saturday night."

He gave her a considering look. "I already made a promise with somebody else."

"Related to being a pastor?" She knew she was pushing, but he kinda just asked her out on a date. She felt like she had the right to push.

"No. Not really."

"So you're not counseling anyone on Saturday night?"

"No." He cut his eyes over to her, and their gazes caught and held.

"Is it a date?" Her words were soft, and she hadn't meant to say them. But she didn't want to take them back, because she wanted to know.

His lips flattened and pulled, and her stomach dropped, crawling under the seat.

It was. He didn't even have to answer. But he did.

"Yes."

"Is your daughter going?" She almost tripped over the use of "your." She couldn't even go there, dealing with two different hard things. Her daughter and this man that she couldn't stop thinking about.

"No."

"I think I'll have to decline your invitation for Sunday afternoon." She took a shaky breath, pulling her eyes away. They pulled up to the barn, and he stopped a second later. Unbuckling her belt, she jumped out without saying anything more.

She had no right to be angry. She had no right to him at all. It was a chant in her head, over and over. Eventually she'd believe it.

Except, he'd asked her out on a picnic. He'd gotten her hopes up, then dashed them.

As she started around the front of the truck, a man walked out of the barn. Tall and straight, wearing worn jeans, cowboy boots, a cowboy hat, and a Western-style shirt, all he needed was a horse and chaps for her to think he was a real cowboy.

It had to be Wilder from North Dakota. She braced herself, trying to settle her emotions. She wouldn't be upset with Deacon; he had been nothing but nice to her, getting her this opportunity, and she wasn't going to screw it up because of some annoying emotions.

Putting a smile on her face, she walked forward with her hand out.

Chapter 7

Two and half hours later, Blair finally shook Wilder's hand, saying a few parting words, and headed toward Deacon's truck.

Deacon had settled down on the ground by the front wheel and had his Bible out, reading and taking notes.

The length of time that she spent there boded well for her, he thought. She'd even come back and gotten her toolbox with all her farrier tools and equipment in it. She'd smiled at him and given him a little thumbs-up on her way past.

He stood up, brushing himself off and adjusting his hat, which he'd pulled down to shade his eyes.

Yeah. He was pretty sure she got the job.

He waved a hand as Wilder called a farewell; Deacon returned it.

He only hesitated for a minute before taking two steps to meet Blair and taking her toolbox from her. She gave him a look as he took it, which he met with a mildly challenging one of his own.

He didn't understand what was so controversial about a man wanting to do something nice for a woman. It wasn't because he didn't think she could do it. Obviously, she could. She'd gotten it out and carried it over to the barn and back. He just wanted to be nice.

He appreciated that she let him.

He set it in carefully and climbed into the cab of the truck. She was already in with her seatbelt on.

He started it before he spoke. "Do you mind if we go straight to my house?" He put the truck in reverse and backed away from the barn. "I wasn't expecting it to take this long, and I need to get changed. I can show up at Wilder's like this, but I probably can't show up for counseling in these dirty clothes."

Blair bit her lip as she looked over at him. "I'm so sorry. If I'd realized it was going to take that long, I would have told you to go ahead and go. You could've come back and picked me up. Do you live far from here?"

Growing up in town, she probably wasn't as familiar about who owned the farms scattered out around.

"Twenty minutes. Then it'll take another twenty minutes to get to town. I've already called my mom, and she's keeping Tinsley."

Blair nodded, still picking at her seatbelt.

"You didn't know how long it would take. Don't worry about it." Deacon put the truck in drive and started the long trek out the driveway. He grinned over at her. "It must have gone well. You were smiling until you started biting your lip."

Her smile came back, full-on, and he was reminded again why she was so popular in high school. Beautiful any time, she was stunning when she smiled. Stunning as in he had to remember to take his eyes off her and watch where he was going on the road.

"He's going to hire me!" She bounced a little on the seat, and he had to smile. Words wouldn't come because she reminded him so much of Tinsley. From the way her chin pointed, to the way her mouth tilted up, and even the childish way she bounced on the seat.

"It's like having my daughter in the seat beside me."

He thought his words were flippant and casual, but she jerked her head to him, her eyes wide, her mouth open before it pursed.

"I was kidding. That isn't a bad thing."

It looked like she was deliberately calming herself, taking a deep breath and flexing her fingers before relaxing them in her lap. "Of course. I'm sorry. I knew you were joking."

"Wow. Okay. I love my daughter more than anything, and I meant it as a huge compliment. I'm sorry it came out wrong."

"No. I'm sorry. It was all me." Her voice trailed off.

Unable to figure out what he'd done, he changed the subject. "You were telling me how it went." He pulled out from the driveway onto the highway. "You got the job... He liked you, then."

"Yes. He had me shoe a horse. That's why I came out and got my tools and equipment. And of course, that's what took so long. I'm sorry you had to wait." Some of the excitement was back in her voice, and it warmed Deacon's heart.

He wasn't sure exactly what was going on with comparing her to Tinsley, but that had really evoked some negative feelings in her.

Blair tucked some hair that had escaped out of her ponytail back behind her ear. "He said that he had been thinking for a while now of hiring an additional farrier to help with the workload. Apparently the one that he's using now, Buzz I think he said his name was, is getting closer to retirement age and had issues with his back anyway. He's not sure what this accident is going to do."

Deacon hooked his elbow on the open window. "I was pretty sure he was gonna take you. But I didn't want to get your hopes up."

"You mean you knew all along?" She crossed her arms over her chest and looked at him.

"No. Of course he had to talk to you. Did he ask for references?"

"He didn't ask if I was in prison, if that's what you're asking."

"I'm not sure Wilder was in town when that all went down. He might've been around, but he wouldn't have known and maybe wouldn't have remembered."

"That's true. Still, gossip travels fast."

"I'm sure people have been talking since you came back, but Wilder isn't one to listen to gossip." Deacon tapped his fingers on the steering wheel. There'd been a question bothering him for a while, and he wondered if he could ask.

Finally, he decided to just ask. "Do we know each other well enough for me to ask you a personal question?"

"How personal is personal? You want to know how much he offered to pay me?" She gave a little sassy shake of her head.

Deacon figured he'd take her up on that. Just to see if she'd tell him. "Yeah. How much?"

"Nope. We don't know each other well enough for that. Plus, you only want to know so you know that I'm giving my tithe on Sunday mornings."

"Oh, that's rich. Funny." He shook his head. "I never even see any of that. The treasurer does that, and I get a little report, but it doesn't have names on it."

"But you could get names if you wanted."

"Probably. I could get the answer to the question that I actually wanted to ask too, because that wasn't it." He shot her a grin. "But I didn't want to ask anyone but you."

"Oh." Her arms dropped from in front of her, and she shoved more stray hair off her face. Her ponytail was definitely the worse for the wear. "Okay. You can ask. With the assumption and understanding that I don't have to tell."

"Fair enough." He turned into his driveway, going slightly faster than he had down Wilder's. He really was going to be late if he didn't get a move on. But he wasn't in such a hurry that he kept from saying what he'd wanted to say to Blair for a while. "I want to know what you went to prison for."

He let the words hang in the air, in the quiet of the cab, with the wind not blowing through anymore since they'd slowed down.

He kept his head straight ahead, but he could see out of his peripheral vision that she didn't look at him. Her head faced forward, and her hands were completely still in her lap. She didn't remind him of Tinsley anymore.

He thought maybe he'd really overstepped his bounds, and he kind of regretted saying anything because they'd been getting along so well.

"You don't have to tell me, of course. I could ask my mom, or any of my brothers, or even Pastor Wyatt would tell me." He adjusted his grip on the steering wheel and turned his head. "But I wanted to ask you."

She still stared straight out the windshield. He took one hand, with one finger, and poked her in the shoulder gently. She jerked her head over, her brows drawn, but when she saw the look on his face, maybe the little smile, her expression softened.

"I get that it's not something you want to talk about. And I can respect that. Please don't think you have to answer."

"I will. I was just trying to figure out how to say it. It's not exactly my proudest moment."

"I get that. I said you don't have to tell me."

"I want to. You deserve to know. You stuck your neck out for me today, and you still don't know whether I'm actually going to do what I said I was gonna do or whether I'm going to make you look like an idiot. I appreciate it."

"Hey, we had a deal. I will keep my end of it."

"And I'll keep mine. But I'll also tell you why I went to prison." Her voice trailed off as his house came into sight. It wasn't anything to write home about, just a small ranch home next to a big pole building where he kept some equipment for the crop farming that he did. "How about I'll tell you about it on the way in to church?"

"Yeah, that will work. I'm running a little late anyway."

"No animals?"

"No. I'm not home enough to take care of them. Working two jobs, plus with Tinsley... We have a dog and a few cats running around."

"I just think animals when I think farm."

"Everybody does. I know a lot of farms don't even have any animals. Animals tie you down. You can't go anywhere. Because you gotta take care of them and feed them. A lot easier to just put the tractor in the shed, and it's good until the next time you need it."

She nodded. "I've lived here all my life, and I had no idea you live back here. This isn't the house you grew up in though, right?"

"No, although that's not very far away. We all live around close. Maybe my parents wish that we moved a little further away or that the apple dropped a little further from the tree."

They laughed.

"I highly doubt it. I'm pretty sure I heard your mother saying yesterday in church that she just loved being able to see her grandkids all the time as she picked them up from kids' club."

"You're right. I think she does love it." He pulled in front of the house and felt a little uncomfortable for the first time. "You're welcome to come in and make yourself at home." It wasn't an invitation that he made very many times in his life to a woman.

"Thanks. I'm kinda thirsty."

"Come on in. I'll get you a drink."

BLAIR STOOD IN THE living room in Deacon's house, staring at the picture above the mantle. From the look of it, it wasn't taken that long ago, and it was of Deacon, along with the little girl who had to be Tinsley. She was beautiful.

All Blair could do was stare.

Yesterday in church, she'd tried to catch a glimpse of her, but she'd been with the younger kids, and Blair had the older elementary. Being that it was her first time teaching, it was all she could do to try to keep herself afloat. Plus, if she was going to see Tinsley, she wasn't sure she wanted it to happen in front of a whole lot of other people. She wasn't sure she could hold herself together.

Just staring at the picture made her whole torso cramp. She wanted to wrap her arms around her stomach and bend over hugging herself to ease the pain.

Thinking about how much she missed, how much she'd screwed up, how much she wished things had been different. It hurt her heart yet made her chest expand in a beautiful way, thinking that the sweet little girl was a part of her.

There wasn't anything that could make her feel better for the things she'd missed, but seeing Deacon's hand on the skinny shoulder, and looking at the bright eyes and happy smile of the little girl in the picture, tracing Deacon's body line as he leaned just a little into her, she could tell there was nothing in the world more important to Deacon than his daughter.

It was a moving picture.

It confirmed over and over again in her heart that she had made the right choice. For herself and for Tinsley.

Maybe not for Deacon. If Tinsley hadn't been dropped off at the church that day, Deacon wouldn't be half killing himself working a regular job, farming, and basically volunteering full-time as the assistant pastor.

He'd be the pastor.

Blair had taken that from him.

She half suspected Deacon would say it was worth it. Just from the look on his face and the way his body canted toward his daughter in the picture. But it didn't matter. Even if the ending had been good, the way she'd gone about it had been wrong.

"That's Tinsley."

Deacon's voice from behind her startled her, and she turned quickly, as though caught doing something she shouldn't be. But his eyes were on the picture. "Tinsley is the best thing that ever happened to me."

She blinked several times quickly and tried to process what he just said. "My mom said that you would have been ordained except Tinsley showed up and caused a ruckus, and several pastors who were there to vote on your ordination changed their minds until further investigation because they felt like you'd withheld information from them." She'd heard it often enough. Her mom had gone on and on about it for a long time. Blair had never stopped her. It was like punishment over time. But he kept Tinsley, and that was the important thing.

"Sometimes what feels like the worst thing that could happen to you is the best in the end. We just don't see things the way God sees them sometimes. Or maybe we just don't see the end the way God sees it."

"So you don't resent her?"

"Not at all." He turned, and his eyes, deep blue brought out by the blue plaid button-down he wore, searched her face. "After the personal questions I've asked you, I'm surprised. Usually by now, people have asked me if she was really mine. You don't seem curious."

Oh boy. She turned her head quickly and stared at the picture. She didn't want to lie. She put that kind of life behind her. But what could she say?

The truth?

No. She wasn't ready. She wasn't ready for the explosion. Although, she was hopeful. If Deacon thought that Tinsley was the best thing that ever happened to him, he might not be angry at her. The town might not lynch her because she'd ruined the life of one of their favorite sons. But it would create a mess. And there was Tinsley to consider in all of this. Was it even best for Tinsley to know that she was her mom? That her mom was in town. How would that work?

There were too many unknowns, too many things she wasn't sure of, too many things she was ashamed of. She couldn't come out with the truth yet.

"I guess I'm curious about the story, but I kinda feel like you're not the kind of man that would have a child like that."

There. It was the truth. Although if she hadn't known what the exact truth about Tinsley was, she might have wondered.

Deacon, however, seemed satisfied with her answer. "Maybe you've given me more credit than I deserve."

"I don't think so. You have the reputation for a reason. And a good reputation is much harder to build than a bad one."

"'A good name is rather to be chosen than great riches.'"

She grunted. "I recognize the quote, that it comes from the Bible, but I don't know where."

"Proverbs, but it doesn't matter. If you recognize it is Bible, that's all you need."

She swallowed, suddenly aware that he was standing close, close enough that she could close the distance with the step. As she was suddenly tempted to do.

No. She wasn't even going to go there. Their reputations went off in opposite directions, and being with her would ruin his.

Especially now, with Pastor Wyatt potentially needing to take time off to take care of his sick wife, Deacon didn't need a complication like her.

"Now that you've seen her, did you change your mind about going on a picnic with her on Sunday afternoon?"

Her heart stumbled. He'd surprised her. She hadn't expected to be asked the first time; she definitely didn't expect to be asked again.

"It wasn't Tinsley." She didn't often get the opportunity to say her daughter's name out loud, and it felt good. But she shifted, taking a small step back, putting some space between them, and letting him know she didn't appreciate him taking her lightly.

Deacon put a hand behind his neck and rubbed. "There is a woman in the church who has six children. She lost her husband last fall. Miss Lynette saw that she needed a husband, and she saw me, thinking I needed a wife. She wanted us to get together." He blew out a breath and dropped his hand. "I told her I would try. I've already met with her once at the park. With all of our kids running around. Neither one of us was very interested. We decided it might be different if it was just us.

That's how I came to be taking her out Saturday night. We're not going anywhere fancy or doing anything crazy. I just have to do what I told Miss Lynette I would do."

"That's still not fair to one of us. That you're planning on taking someone out Saturday night and someone else out on Sunday afternoon."

"Inez and I aren't exclusive. It's not that way. And I don't think she's any more interested in me than I am in her. Other than I would be a good dad and she would be a good mom. It's hardly a reason to get married."

People get married for stupider reasons. Blair crossed her arms over her chest and turned back to the wall, looking at the picture of the father and his daughter.

So many years. So many wasted years.

"Still. You're not the kind of man that would date two women at once."

"Who said anything about a date? I was going to take you on a picnic with my daughter. That's not a date."

If anyone had told Blair that Deacon could make her blush, she would've argued with them and told them it was impossible. But her cheeks were heating. Had she really read too much into that?

Her eyes narrowed. The space that she had placed between them disappeared as she took a step forward. "Really? You didn't mean it as a date?"

His cocky look and cheeky grin had been replaced with a tightening around his mouth, and his Adam's apple bobbed. "Blair?"

"Deacon?" she imitated. It was exactly like she thought. He was teasing her, and she tried to turn the tables on him. But he was just as innocent as he seemed, and she was just as not. If he wanted to play this game, she would win.

Her hand stopped on the way up to rest beneath his collarbone.

What was she doing?

She wasn't this person anymore. Not with anyone, but especially not with Deacon. She dropped her hand and turned away. "Are you ready to go? I thought we were going to be late?"

"Blair?"

"Forget it, Deacon. Whatever you're thinking, just forget it. There's nothing here. You're treading on thin ice even trying to be friends with me. Just stay back."

She walked across the room and out the door without looking back at him.

Chapter 8

The ride to the church was quiet. Deacon could have kicked himself for pushing so hard. What was he even thinking? Blair was right; there was no future for them. Not really. She was only expecting to stay long enough to help her mom, anyway.

Obviously, she wasn't interested. He'd been pretty obvious that he was, and she'd turned him down flat.

She had a ton more experience than he did, and she probably saw him for the awkward loser that he was.

He'd spent a lot of time trying to learn the Bible, and learning to do what the Lord wanted him to, but hardly any thinking about what he might need to say to a woman in order to convince her to take a chance on him.

He'd depended on God to bring his wife into his life. He supposed, in hindsight since everything was always more clear that way, that God didn't typically do everything. He expected the human he was helping to have a little bit of a brain. That's why God gave it to them after all.

God helps those who help themselves.

It wasn't exactly a Bible verse but was based on biblical teaching. Maybe more applicable would be "whatsoever thy hand findeth to do, do it with thy might." Or maybe Solomon knew what he was talking about when he wrote in Proverbs that one of the wonders of the world was "the way of a man with a maid."

Deacon wished to spend a little more time studying that verse and figuring out what exactly the way of a man with a maid was.

So he could use some of it on Blair.

Too late though. The lady had been clear. She didn't want him.

As he pulled into the church, he figured he better break the silence. "We're meeting with Kendra. She's sixteen. I would like your word that anything that's said in the church today won't leave the church. You don't even have to sit close. She and I will sit on different pews, with me turned around facing her. You can sit anywhere, but stay in the sanctuary, please."

"I'll keep an eye on you but not an ear. Is that right?"

He tilted his head over at her. "Does that mean you're not mad at me anymore? If you're making jokes?"

"I wasn't mad at you to begin with. I was more mad at myself."

"Mad at yourself? Why?"

She threw a hand in the air before it came down and slapped her leg. "How can you ask that? You know what I've done in the past. How can you even ask why I might be mad at myself?"

"I don't know how everything you've done had anything to do with what happened between us today."

"It has everything to do with it. And you know it. Especially for you, and who you are."

His brows drew down, but a dark blue car pulled in beside them. "That's her. I really would like to talk to you some more. If you won't do a picnic by the river, maybe you could set the parameters."

"Just let it go." She jerked the latch on her door and started to push it open.

"Maybe I don't want to let it go."

She put a leg out, and he wanted to grab her and stop her, but he fisted his hands in his lap instead. He had to let her go.

As she slid out, she turned her head over her shoulder. "Maybe it doesn't matter what you want."

She'd certainly rejected him enough for one day.

He had to try to get his head in the game, thinking about Kendra and the issues that she was having with her parents, and different verses in the Bible that he might need to go to, trying to have them on the tip of his tongue so that he was ready to answer any questions she might have.

Blair was true to her word. She stayed close enough to see but not hear.

Maybe because of her discretion, the counseling session went well. He thought anyway. Kendra was coming along and seemed to accept Blair much better than Lynette, who was a very godly woman but did come on a little strong.

Kendra's relationship with her parents was still rocky, but as he spoke to her, she wasn't quite as rebellious about it as she had been.

"Okay. I'll see you again next week."

"Oh, you will. My parents aren't going to let me out of it."

"Sorry about your luck," he said with a benign smile, admiring her parents for doing the hard thing. It was a lot easier to just let your kid do whatever she wanted to do than to actually make her do something hard, like go see the assistant pastor and take counseling.

It would be a struggle at home, he was sure.

Kendra jerked her head at Blair. "Is that the girl from town that was in prison?"

Deacon raised a brow as he gathered up his Bible but didn't say anything. He knew that had probably made Kendra more relaxed, but he wasn't going to talk about it with her.

"My parents said she was back in Cowboy Crossing. What a hick town. I don't know why anybody would leave and come back."

"There's a lot of things to love about a small town. One would be the fact that you don't really need to lock your doors at night."

She was too young to appreciate a small town. Some kids seemed to grow up, content where they were. And others, like Kendra, couldn't wait to leave, stretch their wings, and make their mark on the world. Never content with the quiet, peaceful stillness that he treasured so highly.

"So, is she the ex-con or not?" Kendra asked. Again.

Deacon stood. "I'll see you next week."

"She must be. Don't know why you're being so weird about it though. If she served time in prison, she served time in prison. No point pretending she didn't."

"I am. I'm the ex-con." Blair had come down the middle aisle and now stood beside Kendra's pew. "I'm Blair." She held her hand out.

Kendra looked at it for a minute, and Deacon had to swallow hard and clench his fist. Tempted, if Kendra said anything unkind to Blair, to grab a hold of the little squirt's throat. He didn't like Blair calling herself an ex-con either. It might be true, but she didn't need to put herself down.

After what felt like a really long time to Deacon, Kendra lifted her hand up. "I'm Kendra."

She seemed to look Blair up and down. Deacon bit his tongue, frustrated that this must be what Blair dealt with all the time, the downturned look, the idea that she wasn't good enough, having prison thrown up in her face.

He realized she'd never told him what she'd done. He couldn't believe he'd forgotten. He supposed it was because of all the rejections.

"It's nice to meet you, Kendra. I think the whole reason that your parents are sending you to Deacon is to keep you from being an ex-con. So if you think it's a bad thing, maybe you might think about listening to him."

She dropped Kendra's hand and kept walking up the aisle toward the altar where she knelt, putting her head on the railing.

Deacon turned back to Kendra who was still staring at Blair.

"I know that," she said in a much softer voice than she had been using. More humble. "But it never sunk in, not like it did just now. I get it." Her face turned toward Deacon. "That would never happen to me."

"I'm pretty sure if you talk to her, Blair will tell you that she thought the exact same thing. Did your mom tell you that along with a prison sentence, Blair was a cheerleader and homecoming queen? She was popular in school. Everyone loved her. No one would have said it could happen to her."

Kendra nodded, digesting Deacon's words. Deacon didn't turn around, but he hadn't heard Blair stand, and he assumed she was still kneeling at the altar. He'd spent a lot of hours there himself. He wanted to turn and go and pray with her, but he could hardly walk away from Kendra.

"'Pride goeth before destruction, and a haughty spirit before a fall.' Don't ever think that it couldn't happen to you."

That was exactly why Blair was here today. He couldn't imagine doing anything inappropriate with Kendra. There was absolutely zero temptation for him. But it was so easy to think that it couldn't happen to him. And he didn't want to have that haughty spirit that went before a fall.

"I'll see you next week, Mr. Hudson." Kendra waved at him and walked off.

Deacon waited until she was out of church and he heard the door close before he turned. Blair was still there, and her back shook like she was crying.

Knowing he still had to be careful, Deacon walked down the aisle and knelt beside her. He put one hand on her shoulder and whispered a prayer in the stillness of the sanctuary.

Her shoulder stiffened when he touched it but relaxed under the words he said to the Almighty.

He fell silent, pleading with the Lord to heal whatever heartache she had, most of it stemming from mistakes of the past, he would guess. It was frustrating that things one did in one's youth could close doors to opportunities for the rest of one's life.

Blair hadn't had to tell him, but being a farrier was a great career for her, because she would never have to fill out an application and mark down that she'd been incarcerated.

She stirred under his hand, which was still on her back, lifting her tearstained face. "I'm sorry. I'm holding you up. You don't have to stay."

"You're not holding me up. There's nowhere else I want to be."

"There's got to be a million places you'd rather be than sitting beside me while I bawl my eyes out." She grabbed a tissue from the box behind the rail, intended for that purpose, and wiped her eyes and blew her nose. "I promised to tell you why I went to prison."

"I wanted you to tell me Sunday afternoon down by the creek."

"I don't want to ruin a good Sunday afternoon."

"That's not going to ruin anything."

"Maybe not for you. You're not the one who lived it."

"It's under the bridge."

Her lips flattened, and she turned away. "I know that. Sometimes it just doesn't feel that way."

"It's not God that needs to forgive you. It's you that needs to forgive yourself. Let it go."

"How can I forgive myself when everyone I see reminds me that I'm a failure? It feels like everything I do comes back to that. Every person I meet, I can see it in their eyes. Being in Cowboy Crossing is especially bad. At least in the town I was living in, it wasn't something that every single person knew. Now, I can't pump gas, can't go the grocery store, can't teach kids' club at church without people looking at me and accusing me even if they don't say anything. It's the way they pull their kids away from me or the way they say hi and keep walking."

"The Bible says 'whatsoever a man soweth that shall he also reap.'"

"That's the first time I've ever wanted to tell you to shut up."

He didn't flinch. "Start planting a different crop. You have to get through the bad harvest, and then you start reaping the good."

She put her head down. "I'm sorry." Her breath was fast, like she'd been running, but her shoulders were slumped.

He wanted nothing more than to fix everything for her. To touch her, share the pain she was feeling. He hated that she had to take it alone.

"You're right. That's what turning over a new leaf is. Going down a different path. Planting a different crop. Never thought about it like that. Because you're right, you reap what you sow. Yet, you have the option to start sowing something different anytime."

"Exactly. You still have the bad crop in the ground. And you might always get a little of that crop, but every year, it gets better and better."

"Leave it to a Missouri farm boy to have such a good grasp on the concept of sowing and reaping."

Deacon grunted. "It's what I love."

"I thought you loved being a pastor? I thought that was your dream?"

"Can I be both? Jesus was a carpenter, right? Paul was a tentmaker."

"That's true."

"I'm not sure if it's biblical for a man to do nothing but preach. Although, I gotta say it'd be easier on my pocketbook."

She laughed. "You might be a preacher, but I can't picture you with a pocketbook."

"Tinsley's had more than a few, usually bright pink, and trust me, I've carried a pocketbook."

Her smile seemed sad, and he remembered earlier that she'd been upset when he talked about Tinsley.

"Why does that happen?"

"What?" she asked, grabbing another tissue and blowing her nose again.

"When I say something about Tinsley, it's like you withdraw into a shell."

She shrugged and looked away.

"Don't lie."

Her head snapped back around. "I didn't need that reminder. I didn't lie, and I wouldn't."

"There's something going on."

"Maybe there is. But maybe I don't want to talk about it. Maybe that's not something I'm going to tell you. Whether you're a pastor or not." By the time she was done, she seemed very defensive, and he knew he needed to back off again.

"I'm sorry. You're right. None of my business. You don't have to tell me anything."

"I'm sorry. It is something I'm...sensitive about. Maybe someday." She looked kind of hopeful and pushed to her feet. "I think I've held you up long enough."

"I told you I don't have anywhere else to go. There's nowhere I'd rather be." He pushed up with her. "We on for Sunday? You're gonna tell me about what happened, Tinsley's gonna play in the creek, and we'll eat some good picnic food that my mom will be thrilled to make. Sound like a deal?"

"I think I've already said no to that three times."

"Then this is the time you say yes."

She looked down to the tissue in her hand, like it held the answers to the hard questions of the universe. "I don't think it's a good idea."

He waited, holding his breath. He could feel her wavering.

"Yes. I'll go on a picnic Sunday afternoon with you."

He had to smile. What else could he do? "Thanks."

Chapter 9

"I had such a good day, I think we should go out to eat." Blair's mom sat on the porch swing, holding Mr. Rogers in their lap.

Blair watched her mom stroke the cat. She hadn't wanted to go anywhere today. She didn't want to take the chance of seeing Deacon with his date. Even if he said they really didn't mean anything, it wasn't something she wanted to be face-to-face with.

She couldn't like him, and she knew he would never be interested in someone with a past like hers, except...yesterday it almost seemed like he had been.

He really insisted about taking her to the creek. Almost like he really wanted her to go. Maybe he just wanted her to be around Tinsley, so he could try to figure out what the deal was. That made her nervous. She had come home for her mom, and because she was hoping to make things right, but she had no idea of what to do.

She definitely hadn't thought that one through. Like so much of her life.

That got her into trouble more times than she could count. Having a grain of an idea, but no thought as to how she was going to see it through.

There was nothing she could do to make up for Deacon's loss, and according to Deacon, he didn't even feel like he'd lost anything now. Although at the time he had.

The whispers she heard around town made her feel like the townspeople still felt like he lost something too.

"Are you sure you feel up to it, Mom?" *Please say no, please say no.*

"This is the best day I've had in weeks. Yes. Let's go do something. Too bad you weren't teaching kids' club tonight. I could definitely do it with you."

"Or teaching Miss Lynette's Sunday school class, you could do that with me too."

"Blair, I can't tell you how proud I am of you. I love the way you stepped up and are helping Deacon out. He's such a nice boy."

"Mom, you're not being subtle."

"I wasn't trying to be, honey. I'll be obvious. Deacon would make you an excellent husband."

"Mom. That might be true. But I would not make him an excellent wife. That's the rub."

"But look at you. You're spending every evening home with your sick mom, teaching Wednesday night kids' club and Sunday school starting this Sunday, and did I hear that you were supposed to be making supper for Billie Joe Burns who just had a baby?"

"I'm going to order something at the diner and take it to her family. You know as well as I do if I try to cook supper, I'm going to burn it."

"You keep trying, baby, you'll get it. Everybody has to start somewhere." Mr. Rogers pushed his head into her mother's hand, and her mother scratched his ears.

It just amazed Blair that some days her mother didn't seem to be able to use her fingers hardly at all, and yet today she was running her fingers over the cat and scratching the ears. The disease didn't make any sense to her. Hopefully the doctors would have some ideas when they went to her appointment.

Her mother eyed her critically. "Are you going to go like that?"

Blair looked down at her outfit, still leaning against the porch post. "What's wrong with this?" She was wearing jeans, a shirt, and flip-flops. It wasn't fancy, but it wasn't like she was wrapped in a towel.

Her mother stroked the cat, keeping her face down. "Oh, nothing. If that's what you want to go in."

"If you want me to change, why don't you just say so? Although if we're just going to the diner, nobody dresses up there." Surely Deacon wouldn't take Inez to the diner. There were other, nicer places to go.

"You could put on a clean pair of jeans, or a skirt would be even better. But hey, if you want to go like that, go ahead."

"You know what, Mom, I'll just go do that. You need me to bring you anything down?"

"No, thank you," her mom said with a smug look, still stroking Mr. Rogers.

Blair let out an aggravated sigh. Why couldn't her mom have just said, *hey, Blair, want to go change your clothes*? Why did she have to do the whole psychological manipulation thing?

A little voice in her head told her that her mom did it because she loved her and didn't want to boss her around. It was her way of making a suggestion without being bossy. Maybe not the way Blair wanted her to do it, but she'd finally gotten to the point in her life where she was just thankful to have her mother, despite her shortcomings. Or maybe her mother's shortcomings magnified her own.

She put on something that she thought her mom might approve of before taking a look at her hair and fixing that as well.

If Deacon really was out on a date, and she did run into him, she didn't want to look like yesterday's leftovers. She could thank her mom for that.

If her mom walked a little slower, if she seemed to tire out more easily, if she held on to Blair's elbow when she didn't used to, Blair was still happy that she could step out with her. She shouldn't even have given her a hard time. It was a beautiful evening, with the good smells of summer all around. The corn was just starting to tassel in the fields surrounding their town, and she loved that smell of pollen and growing grain and earth and hard work and pride. There couldn't be anything to compare to it anywhere else in the world.

They had to walk by the park on their way to the diner, and there were children laughing and swinging and playing on the monkey bars.

Blair always tried to avoid scenes like these, because they tugged at her heartstrings. If she'd made different choices, if she'd been smarter with her life, she might have had kids who were playing in the park on a summer evening while she sat on a park bench holding her husband's hand and talking about life and family and the vacation they were going to take that year.

She put her hand over her mother's hand that was tucked in the crook of her elbow and patted her mother's fingers.

"What's the matter, honey?" her mother asked.

"Nothing. I guess I was just thinking that I would like in one way to have children playing on the swing right now, but if I did, then I wouldn't be walking down the street with you."

"That's right, sweetie." Her mother took a breath and seemed to slow down a little. "There is always a bright spot. You just have to find it." Her fingers tightened on Blair's arm as she crossed a crack in the sidewalk. "That's what God means when he came up with 'whatsoever things are true, whatsoever things are pure, whatsoever things are right…think on these things.'"

"I guess that's the Bible's version of positive thinking," Blair said a little flippantly, unwilling to be too contemplative or serious. She didn't want to be sad.

"That makes sense. God knows because he made us."

They walked in silence for a little bit. Blair again realized that maybe she missed out on a lot of the wisdom that her mom had over the years.

"Hey, Mom?"

"What is it, sweetie?"

"I'm sorry." Blair turned and looked at her mom, stopping on the sidewalk and looking down at the woman who had loved her and prayed for her and begged her to not do the stupid things that she'd insisted on doing. "I'm sorry about all the heartache I caused you. I'm sorry I don't listen. I'm sorry you cried over me. I wish I could go back and change."

Blair tried to swallow around the knot in her throat. She hadn't meant to apologize tonight, hadn't even thought about it, but that apology had been a long time coming. Her mother deserved that and a lot more.

"Don't you worry about it, sweetheart. You're right. There were a lot of late nights, a lot of tears, a lot of time on my knees begging God for you. But you know..." Her mom tilted her head and smiled tremulously. "It was hard, true. But it brought me so much closer to the Lord. In a way I needed. It wasn't fun, and it wasn't easy, but don't apologize for doing something that made me a better person."

Blair wiped her cheeks, first one, then the other. "I don't deserve your forgiveness, Mom."

"You have it anyway."

Her mom's loving arms came around her, and it was hard to think of anything else that could make her feel more loved or accepted than a hug from her mom, knowing she was forgiven.

She buried her nose in her mom's neck and breathed in the scent that had been so familiar since childhood. It hadn't changed for as long as she could remember. She didn't even know what made up that scent. It was just the perfect blend of love and toughness and total blind faith in a God she couldn't see.

"I never doubted that God would bring you back. I just didn't know when." Her mom patted her, and Blair squeezed her tight, so glad her mom had never given up on her.

They stood like that for a while, until her mom finally said, "Come on. I'm hungry. Let's go get ourselves something to eat."

DEACON SAT ACROSS FROM Inez in a side booth in the diner. Amy had just brought their food, and Inez thanked her politely.

Demure and sweet, despite having six children, Inez would make some man an excellent wife. Deacon wished he could be more interested.

"It's so nice to be able to eat in peace and quiet. Thank you so much for bringing me." Inez smiled sweetly before she took a bite of her spaghetti.

He had to add grateful to the last two. Her virtues added up, but he felt bored and restless and couldn't keep from looking out the window even though he knew Blair would be home with her mother and there was no chance of seeing her.

He brought his eyes back to his food and picked up his fork. He should be making some kind of polite conversation, but he couldn't think of anything to say.

He swallowed the mashed potatoes he'd just put in his mouth. "The weather was nice today."

Inez nodded. "Yes. Lots of sun."

"I like sunny days."

"Me too. Sunny days are really nice."

"Rainy days are good too."

"That's true. Rain is good."

Deacon looked at his plate. They'd pretty much exhausted conversation about the weather unless he wanted to talk about snow. Since it was summer, that seemed dumb.

What else was there? He put food in his mouth so he'd have an excuse to not talk to her again while he tried to figure out what else in the world they could talk about. As he chewed his hamburger, he looked out the window.

He straightened. His heartbeat sped up. His throat closed, and he coughed so he didn't choke on his meat. He leaned over, trying not to be obtrusive about it, but he was pretty sure that was Blair and her mother, and they were walking on the sidewalk next to the building. They went past a light pole, came out again, and yeah, it was them.

He forgot all about the sandwich in his hand because he was pretty sure they were about to walk into the diner.

"What is it?" Inez started to turn around.

Man. He was the worst date ever.

"It's Blair, and she's with her mother. I don't think I've seen her mother out for several weeks." That was sad.

He needed to level with Inez.

But he also needed to pay attention to her. She was his date.

"Oh." Inez nodded. "Mrs. Dixon used to do so much in the church. So sad that she got sick."

"Yeah." He took a tighter hold on the sandwich, but he didn't lift it to his mouth. "Inez, I think you're really sweet, and I think you need help with your children, and I hope you get it, but I don't think that you're any more interested in marrying me than I am in marrying you. Am I wrong about that?"

He didn't know how else to say it. He just needed to be clear. There was a slight downturn to Inez's lips, but then her smile came back, brighter than before. Relieved.

"This has been awkward. It wasn't any better than before when we had our kids running around. I'm sorry I wasted two evenings for you."

Man, he hated that she put it like that. "You didn't waste my time. It was me wasting yours. You're busy with your family to take care of, and you have better things to do than hang around the likes of me, who has the manners of a rhinoceros."

Inez smiled a little; her cheeks turned pink. "I saw you looking at Blair the last time we were together, and it reminded me of the way Clyde used to look at me before we were married. I knew then that this wasn't going to work. Because you're in love with someone else."

Deacon wanted to deny it immediately. He was infatuated with Blair, but he didn't love her.

At least he thought that was the way it was.

Inez had let him off the hook, but he still didn't like the fact that he couldn't keep his eyes from tracking Blair as she came in the door with her mom and walked in the opposite direction, sitting down at a booth on the other side of the diner.

She looked out the window, and he doubted that she knew he was here. Although she knew he was going out, and he was just as likely to be here as anywhere else in town.

She must not have cared whether she saw him or not.

He faced Inez. "I don't deserve your kindness, in spite of my rudeness, but I appreciate it."

Inez leaned forward, with a little secret smile on her face, and turned her head to look toward Blair. "Is there anything I can help you with? I could bump into you when she's walking by and push you into her."

She turned to look at him with a conspiratorial smile. He had to grin.

"I don't think this is what you thought you were going to be doing on your date with me tonight. Helping me get another girl."

"Blair deserves a good turn. I think she made some bad decisions that she regrets."

Another point in Inez's favor. The woman was almost a saint. She was one of those rare people who could look past the surface and into someone's heart.

"A couple of my children had her for junior church on Wednesday, and they loved her. They said she was fun, but when I asked what they learned, they could also tell me. To me, that's the mark of a good teacher."

Deacon had figured as much. Blair was a natural. But he appreciated the words coming from Inez.

Amy bustled over to Blair and her mother's table. They were sitting across the diner, but Deacon could still tell by her body language that she thought Blair was beneath her. It had certainly taken her long enough to go over and wait on their table.

Amy hurried away, and he stopped watching her as two guys who were sitting two tables down from Blair's got up and sauntered over.

He turned to Inez who was calmly eating, currently enjoying her peace and quiet. He was glad for that. "Will you excuse me for a moment, please?"

Her eyes shot up, clear and true. Puzzled. "Sure."

Her brows drew down when she saw his expression, but she didn't ask any questions.

He stood and strode over. He'd never run with a bad crowd, but it wasn't hard to tell when men were bent on mischief.

"Excuse us, Mrs. Dixon, but we thought Blair here might be able to teach us some of the tricks she learned in prison." The guy's voice carried across the room.

"Shut up and leave us alone," Blair snapped at the men before shifting so her shoulder and back were toward them as she looked at her menu. Her voice carried too.

"We were just being friendly."

"Be friendly somewhere else."

"That's no way to treat people who just want to make conversation with you."

"She said leave." Deacon stopped behind the guys.

"Hey." The guy who'd done all the talking lifted his hands up in innocence. "We're just talking to Blair. She was always a good time in high school, and we figured she'd learned a few new things since she'd been in the pen. All those guys around her."

"I was in a ladies' prison."

"Well, that could be interesting too." The guy snickered.

Amy pushed in. The guys moved so she could set the tray down with Mrs. Dixon's and Blair's drinks.

"We'll catch you sometime you're not so busy, Blair." The guy pointed at her—Deacon wasn't sure what that meant—turned around, and walked back to his table.

"I'm sorry about that, Mom," Blair said to her mother.

Amy said, "There's lots of folks in here that don't think you want to teach and do church and Sunday school with the record that you have. I can't say I disagree with them. But I'm to serve you anyway."

Amy's long fingernails clacked on her tray as she picked up the dish of lemons.

Deacon took a step closer and put a hand on the back of the booth behind Blair's head. "That wasn't very nice. If anyone has a problem with who's teaching in the church, they can come see Pastor Wyatt, or they can come see me."

"What kind of example is she for our children?"

"Amy, you don't even have kids," Blair said from where she sat.

Deacon tried not to smile. Obviously, Amy was just following the crowd, not even sure what she was upset about.

"Well, if I did have kids, I would certainly want them to have a better example."

"When you start coming to Sunday school, then maybe you can have a say in who teaches it," Deacon said. "Jesus ascended and left the rest of us poor losers here. There's not a perfect one among us. Whoever teaches Sunday school is not going to be perfect. Whether it's Blair or whether it's someone else. Blair does a great job, and Inez was just telling me—"

"I was just telling him that my children loved her as a teacher and could tell me what their lesson was about. To me, that says they had a good teacher, if they've had fun and they learned something." Inez's voice came from behind Deacon.

He turned and gave her a grateful look. He hadn't treated her the way she should have been treated, but he would be doing her a disservice if he married her. She was right; his heart was firmly stuck on Blair. And he was pretty sure there was no unsticking it at this point.

"Humph." Amy tossed her head. "I'm just telling you what people in here are saying."

"We all know the diner is a hotbed for gossip. Amy, you could stop it. Blair is a great teacher. If you don't think she is, I'm sure the next time she teaches you'd be welcome to come in and sit. Actually, you'd probably be even more welcome to go in and help." Deacon kept his tone level, and he kept his face open, so Amy wouldn't feel like she was being attacked.

Amy tilted her head. "Maybe I'll just do that."

"I'd love it if you do that. We'll put you to work if you come to church." Deacon gave her a half smile, and Amy batted her eyes and smiled back at him.

Amy pointed at their table. "You two better go on over there and sit down and finish your meals, they're going to be cold."

"I think that's a good idea." He didn't want to leave without saying a single word to Blair, but he thought maybe he shouldn't. He was with Inez.

"You ready to walk back over?" he asked Inez.

"Sure." She put her fingertips on the table just touching Blair's hand that was wrapped around her water glass, squeezing tight. "That was true about my children. They really enjoyed whatever structure you built with the desks, and they were very jealous of the little boy that got to sit on the top of it."

Deacon's eyes widened, and he mentally tried to figure out how much insurance the church had.

Maybe he should have a few words with Blair about safety and accidents.

Later.

Chapter 10

Blair and her mother stopped at the park to sit on a bench and watch some kids skateboarding. It was late when they finally walked up the stairs to their house.

"Thanks a lot for going out tonight, Mom. I had a really good time." Her teenage self would never have believed that she would enjoy just walking down the street, eating at the diner, and sitting at the park with her mother of all people. The words were true now. She definitely had a different view of and a higher respect for her mom. Her teenage self was stupid. She had a lot of years to make up for.

Her mother had tried to gently probe about Deacon, but Blair had been pretty tight-lipped. She was enjoying her newfound relationship with her mother, but she wasn't sure what was going on with Deacon, and she didn't want to talk about it.

Her mother took her elbow, and she helped her up the four wide steps to get on the front porch. She should have turned the porch light on, but she had never imagined that they would be out until after dark.

"If you've got a minute, I'd like to talk to you." Deacon's voice came out of the darkness, startling her.

"I'm sorry, I didn't see you." She sounded breathless, because she was. He did that to her. There weren't too many times in her life when a person had come to her defense like Deacon had tonight. Certainly none since she'd gone to prison. His stamp of approval on her meant something.

It also meant something that he was risking his position to have her in the church. If enough people got together, they could both be out. Of course, Deacon wasn't losing any money, but he'd be losing the job he loved.

She supposed Deacon would say God was in control and they should just keep working and not worry about it. Just keep doing right. At one time, she might have rolled her eyes at that. But now, she almost couldn't believe that Deacon was right. Maybe she needed just a little more faith.

"So can you talk?" Deacon prompted.

"I need to go in and help Mom get to bed."

"I can go and get myself to bed. I've been doing it for years now. You stay here and talk to Deacon."

"Mom. I came here for you. I'm going to help you get to bed. If Deacon wants to talk to me, he can wait." Her words sounded a little harsh maybe. But he had been out on a date with another woman earlier in the evening. Two women in one night was a little much for any man, but especially for Deacon. She should turn him down flat.

"I'll wait. Unless you want help."

"No. I can get it."

"Then if it's okay, I'll sit on the swing and wait on you to come out."

"You do that, son," her mother said, grabbing Blair's arm.

BLAIR HADN'T MEANT to take so long. She was actually in a bit of a hurry, which probably made it worse, because she dropped the pills her mom was supposed to take and spent fifteen minutes under the bed looking for one, at the same time trying to keep Mr. Rogers from sniffing around under there. She wasn't sure what the pill she dropped was, or what it would do to a cat, but she figured she better get it picked up.

Then her mom was slow and tired from all the walking that they had done, and her muscles had stiffened up. She had a painful cramp as she was getting in bed, and Blair spent some time massaging her hamstrings.

Finally, she turned the light switch off in her mother's bedroom and hurried downstairs. At least her mom made her change her clothes so she wasn't arriving in dirty stuff, but she hadn't taken the time to fix her hair or shower.

Deacon hadn't said what he wanted to talk about, but she figured iced tea couldn't hurt. So she poured two glasses in the kitchen before she shut the lights off and stepped out on the front porch.

The pole light across the street had come on, illuminating Deacon, rocking gently, one arm stretched out along the back.

"Tea?"

He stood. "Sure. Let me hold it so you can sit down."

"Do I want to sit down?"

"I don't know. Why wouldn't you?" He sounded baffled.

"You didn't tell me what you wanted to talk to me about. Is it bad? I might want to take the bad news standing up." If more people from the church were complaining or if Lynette had gotten worse or if Deacon had lost his job...she didn't want to take any of that sitting down.

"No. I don't think so. I just...I just couldn't stop thinking about you and didn't want to go home without talking to you again."

She sat down on the swing. He handed her a glass of tea and sat down with his own. He didn't lean back and try to put his arm around her, and she appreciated that.

"You were out with Inez tonight. Doesn't it seem a little bit like being a player to be out with one woman in the early evening and out with another later?" She ran her finger over the condensation on the side of the glass. It had bothered her. "I'm not sure I want to be the woman that you spend part of the evening with. Maybe at one time, I was that kind of girl, but not anymore."

"I didn't think that. Honestly, it was just what I said. I wanted to see you. Just didn't want to go to bed without talking to you again."

She closed her eyes against the longing that his words elicited. "This isn't a good idea."

"What? Me seeing you tonight?"

"No. Just you and me in general."

"Why not?" he asked, like he even needed to.

"I don't have to spell it out for you, Deacon. You saw those men in the restaurant today. You heard Amy. You know what they think of me. Don't you realize what a risk you're taking even by having me in the church?"

"I don't consider it a risk."

"You could lose your job. I understand you're not getting paid, but it's what you love to do. You're risking it all."

"Like I said, I don't consider it a risk."

"It's most definitely a risk."

"God knows. If I'm meant to have the job, I will, no matter what forces come against me. And if I'm not, again, it's not a matter of who says what against me. I just have to make sure I'm walking with God, and the rest of the world can do whatever they want. It's not going to affect me."

He was right. Of course.

Maybe someday she'd have faith like that. Or confidence. Confidence that God was leading her, instead of her groping about blindly in the darkness trying to figure out where in the world He was.

"I did get a phone call today from Pastor. Miss Lynette has worse cancer than what they thought. They're doing some more tests, but she has the kind that doesn't respond to chemo. They're trying to get her into some kind of trial, but it doesn't look good for her."

The pain in his voice colored every word. After working so closely with Pastor Wyatt and Miss Lynette, Deacon had to love them both. Without really thinking about it, Blair put her hand on Deacon's knee. "I'm so sorry to hear that. That has to be a hard blow for you."

"It is." He sighed. "I know we're all mortal. We're all going to die. I believe with my whole heart that heaven's so much better than here that if we had the choice to come back after we died, we'd say no. But still, it's so hard to see someone who is so vivacious and so full of life and had been doing so much good struck down."

"It makes me wonder what in the world God's doing. Why would he take someone who's doing so much for Him? Why wouldn't he take me? Why am I not the one with cancer in the hospital dying?" She didn't mean it in a falsely modest way. She just meant that God seemed to be taking one of his very best soldiers out of the battle. Why wouldn't he take a soldier who wasn't fighting in the war?

"No! Don't say that," Deacon said, low and fierce.

Deacon's hand came down and covered hers, warm and rough. She didn't say anything, lost in her thoughts of trying to figure out what in the world God was doing.

"You know, God, the creator of the universe, made galaxies and solar systems. He made things so tiny we will never see them. There's so much about what He's done that I don't understand." Deacon paused. "This is another one of those things. Not that Lynette is sick instead of you. That's not even something I would entertain. But I can't question what God is doing and think that I know better. Because how could I possibly think I know better than someone who created everything we can see? How can I question what He says is best for us?"

"I guess I just can't see far enough ahead to understand how this would be a blessing or would help anyone."

"I can agree with you there. But we don't have God's perspective. He's looking at things from a completely different angle than we are. Kind of the way when Tinsley wants to go play in the river when it's flooding, because it looks like fun. She has no idea of the strength of that current and what it can do to her. I have a different perspective, and I won't let her do it. Does that make sense?"

"I suppose. Like God is our heavenly father, and we're like children not realizing that some of the things we want to do aren't the best for us, and some of the things we don't are."

"Exactly."

"That doesn't mean it's not scary though."

"That's where your verses of comfort come in. It's helpful to have them memorized, because when your doubts come along, and the fear overwhelms you, they're right there."

"It is scary. Seems like there's so much death and destruction. Not just Miss Lynette, but my mom is so much worse than I ever thought she was going to be. I can't think about it, or I'm afraid. It's like I'm falling and I'm all alone."

Deacon was quiet for a minute.

Her hand turned under his, and he threaded his fingers with hers.

They rocked back and forth for a minute, her squeezing his hand, before he started to sing.

What a fellowship, what a joy divine,
Leaning on the everlasting arms.
What a blessedness, what a peace is mine,
Leaning on the everlasting arms.

His voice carried on the night air, perfectly soothing, easing the tight ball in her chest. She laid her head back on the swing and joined him in harmony on the chorus.

Leaning, leaning,
Safe and secure from all alarms;
Leaning, leaning,
Leaning on the everlasting arms.

She wasn't sure of the words to the verse, so her voice trailed off as he kept singing.

What have I to dread, what have I to fear,
Leaning on the everlasting arms.
I have blessed peace with my Lord so near,
Leaning on the everlasting arms.

Again, she joined him. Her voice stronger, her fear and anxiety less. She'd known singing could do that for a person, but she'd forgotten.

Leaning, leaning,

Safe and secure from all alarms;
Leaning, leaning,
Leaning on the everlasting arms.

Their voices quieted, and the night sounds took over again. A car went slowly down the street, and crickets chirped all around them. The springs on the swing creaked with every backward push, and Deacon's hand was still warm and firm and linked with hers.

"Thank you. That made me feel better."

"Based on the verse in Deuteronomy, 'and underneath are the everlasting arms.' Extra soothing words because they were taken straight from the Bible. One of God's precious promises."

"Thank you. Maybe you can send me the reference, and I can look it up."

"I'll do that later." Deacon took two deep breaths, then he said, "I have to cancel our river picnic for tomorrow. That's the main reason I'm here."

"You could have texted me."

His head turned, and his fingers squeezed hers. "Maybe I wanted to see you."

"What's the problem?"

"Mrs. Limbaugh was taken to the hospital with possible appendicitis. I promised her husband when he called that I would go visit her after church tomorrow afternoon."

His thumb traced over the side of her hand. She shivered.

"It was really tempting for me to tell him to forget it. That I couldn't do it tomorrow, because I wanted to be with you. But I couldn't do that."

"Thank you for not. It would make me feel bad to know that you would turn down someone who needed help, in order for you to be with me."

Deacon didn't say anything for a bit, although he shifted slightly, which made her think that he was a little nervous and still had more to say.

Finally, his hand tightened over hers, and he said, "You could go with me."

Her breath caught, and her mouth opened, but no sound came out.

"I know. Exactly what you wanted to do all Sunday afternoon, be at the hospital with someone who has appendicitis. I totally understand if you don't want to do it. I just thought I'd ask."

"As long as my mom's okay, I would love to." She'd go watch turtles race, if it meant being with Deacon. She didn't want to question that right now. They hadn't even really talked about anything, but she felt closer to him than she ever had to anyone else in her life before. Maybe it was the darkness, or the singing, or the fact that his hand was clasped with hers.

That was all, but it was enough.

"My mom will take Tinsley home from church, and I'll leave directly after I'm done talking to everyone. She's in a hospital about an hour away. It has to do with her insurance. I gotta warn you, it's probably all we'll get done tomorrow. When we get back, it will be time to get ready for the evening service."

"I don't care. I'll just need to check on my mom."

"Okay," he said, his thumb brushing lightly over her skin. "It's not romantic, but it's a date."

Chapter 11

There was usually some truth to the old sayings, and Deacon felt like the saying "when it rains, it pours" was completely applicable in his life.

While he was preaching, his phone had buzzed in his suit pocket where he kept it while he preached. He hadn't gotten a chance to check it out yet, since he was still standing in the sanctuary, talking to congregants.

Blair had come in at some point and sat in the back pew. Waiting.

He assumed she'd seen her mother home and made sure she was okay for the afternoon.

It was good to look back and see her eyes on him, see her smile, and know that there was someone pulling for him. He liked the feeling. Maybe he was being fanciful. No matter.

Unfortunately, he'd dealt with several complaints already, and the person standing in front of him was saying the same thing.

It was Mrs. Jones, and her voice was lowered, like she was telling him something she didn't really want to, but yet he highly suspected she'd been looking forward to saying it all morning. "I don't know what Pastor Wyatt was thinking letting that Dixon girl teach Sunday school for Lynette. He should've gotten someone else."

"Why?" He couldn't think of anything else to say. Mrs. Jones had been a member since before he was born, and he didn't always feel like he could argue with ladies like that. Even when he had the Bible on his side.

It was kind of like Gabriel contending with Satan; he needed to let God handle it.

"Don't you know she was in prison?" Mrs. Jones spoke in that same whisper that still managed to contain all of her righteous indignation.

"Apparently, they let her out. They must have felt she wasn't a danger to society anymore."

He knew he was being a little bit flippant, but come on. She had to bury the hatchet sometime.

"You'd better keep a civil tongue in your head, sonny. Don't forget I changed your diapers."

"I didn't mean to be disrespectful, Mrs. Jones. Blair knows she's made some mistakes, and she's working on doing better. However, if you're willing to teach the Sunday school class, I'm sure that she would be willing to give it to you."

Mrs. Jones huffed, and the one long hair on her double chin trembled. "Oh, no. I could never do that. I don't even come to Sunday school anymore. It's just too hard to get out of bed that early when you're as old as I am." Mrs. Jones straightened her considerable girth and took a step back. Offended, apparently. "You need to find someone better."

"Well, I suppose when Jesus comes back, maybe He'll take it over."

"There you are being smart again. I'll be telling Pastor Wyatt what you've been saying to me."

"I'm sorry, again, Mrs. Jones. I'll try to do better." Pastor Wyatt probably would scold him for his flippant comment. But it made him angry that she would talk about Blair like that.

He could understand where she was coming from. He'd understand even more if she actually had a child in the class and was concerned about her child and wanted to talk about perhaps Blair's testimony. But to just complain for the sake of complaining irritated him.

Mrs. Jones reached up and pinched his cheek. "I fed you cereal in the nursery, boy, and wiped your snotty nose. I wanted you for pastor. Still do. You'd make a fine one. But you need to be a little more particular about who you let into the teaching positions. They're responsible for the next generation of Christians. It's a big responsibility. I'm just trying to help you." Mrs. Jones wiggled the hand that pinched his cheek, shaking his whole head, before she dropped it.

For an old lady, she had a strong grip, and his cheek burned.

No matter. He had a few more people to talk to before he could leave.

Fifteen minutes later, he walked to the back of the church, pulling his phone out of his pocket to check the text that he had gotten.

He stopped halfway down the aisle. His stomach wound up tighter than thread on a spool. His heart stomped like a herd of wild buffalo were racing through his chest.

He seemed to be caught under the downpour and couldn't escape it. He lifted his head and saw Blair was already standing up, concern tightening every line of her face as she stepped out of the pew and started slowly toward him.

"What is it?" Her eyes narrowed. "That had to have been really bad news."

"It is. The Fredricksons... I'm sure you know them, they're longtime members here. They were leaving on vacation this morning, and they were in a car accident about the time the services started." He took a breath, steadying his voice and speaking softly. "One of their two daughters was killed, and Mrs. Fredrickson is in critical condition at the same hospital that we will be at." His hand had a death grip on his phone, and his chest felt like it was cased in cement. "I need to get there as fast as possible. They definitely need me."

"Do you still want me?"

"More than ever. But I understand if you don't want to go. This is not going to be an easy afternoon."

"Then I'm with you."

"And I probably will not be very good company. I'm going to be doing a lot of praying on the way there."

"Then I'll pray with you." Her eyes dropped a little. "I don't know if God hears my prayers... They might not do any good."

He took a hold of her shoulder, feeling like he needed to make time for this. "'If I regard iniquity in my heart, God will not hear me.' That means if your sin is gone, then He will. You're just as valuable in God's eyes as I am or anyone else. Don't doubt it."

Her lips turned up in a little smile, and she put her hand over his. "Thank you."

Typically, Deacon tried to obey all the laws of man, including speeding laws. But he had to admit he broke some of them on the way to the hospital that afternoon.

It was just as bad as he thought it would be. Mr. Fredrickson was heartbroken, sobbing in the waiting room, with his daughter gone and his wife barely hanging on. His other daughter had been taken to a relative's house, and Mrs. Fredrickson's parents and some other family members were there. The waiting room was crowded. There was a lot of crying.

Deacon did what he could. Praying with family, holding hands, and giving hugs, each time the doctor came out with an update on Mr. Fredrickson's wife.

Blair stood back, whispering with some of the relatives, hugging Mrs. Fredrickson's mother, and sitting with her for a while. She even slipped out, whispering in his ear before she left that she was going to visit the patient with appendicitis.

Deacon appreciated that since he never made it out of the waiting room the entire afternoon. Finally, it was time to go back for church, and he couldn't stay any longer.

They thanked him profusely for coming, and he promised to come back that evening, after church. They said he didn't have to, but in the next breath, Mr. Fredrickson said he truly would appreciate if he did.

Again, Deacon didn't quite obey all the speeding laws on the way home, but they made it to church on time. Thankfully, Deacon had his message ready, since he only had ten minutes to go over it before it was time to start the service.

He made sure he let out right on time, mostly because he knew he needed to take another hour-long drive and go back to the hospital.

He did notice that Blair slipped out of church twenty minutes before it was over. She'd checked on her mother as soon as they'd gotten home and had been a little late coming into the sanctuary. He couldn't blame her for leaving early. It'd been a long afternoon, and he was exhausted.

But as he walked the last person out, Blair came in holding a bag.

She nodded at the congregant that was leaving, then stepped forward and took hold of his arm. "You're going into your office right now, and you're going to sit down, and you're going to eat this before you do anything else."

He realized he hadn't eaten all day, and he was starving. No wonder he'd felt a little weak and shaky at the end of the service.

"I hope you got enough for two, because you haven't eaten either."

She gave a sad smile. "I did."

"I'm not taking you back with me tonight. It could be pretty long, and I know you need to be with your mom."

She set the bag on his desk and waited until he was sitting in his chair. Pulling the food out, she set it in front of him. "That's fine. It's for the best, I'm sure. I need to go to Wilder's anyway tomorrow, and I can't do that if I've been up all night."

"I really appreciated your help this afternoon." He unwrapped his sandwich, grateful she'd thought of eating. "Tonight will be hard, especially if Mrs. Fredrickson takes any turns for the worse."

"You haven't heard anything?"

"No."

She lifted a brow and crossed her arms over her chest. "Eat."

"Sit."

She flashed a grin. "Is it wrong to smile when other people are hurting so badly?"

"I think we need humor. I've overheard doctors in the hospital at times, and their humor is pretty macabre, but that's what they use to get through the situations they deal with. A merry heart doeth good like a medicine. Too much stress and fear and anxiety will knock you down and knock you out. You need to laugh."

"Good. Because I'm sick of being sad."

"Me too."

"We can laugh a little now."

"Laughter—and food—makes everything better. Thank you." He finished his sandwich before he said anything more. "Maybe we can try for next Sunday afternoon? The picnic by the river?"

Her eyes got big, and she took a breath. "Is that a good idea? We made plans like this today, and look what happened. Do we want to take the chance that we were the instigation for this?"

"I don't wish hardship on anyone, but I wouldn't say that's the chance we were taking." He stopped and looked at her straight for a moment. "I can't tell you how much I appreciated you being there today. Mr. Fredrickson thanked me for bringing you. I appreciate you visiting that other patient. But even more than all that, it was just nice to have someone beside me. You didn't have to, I know not everybody's been super nice to you, but I appreciate it."

She stared at his desk and shifted in her chair before she said softly, "I felt like a fraud. I mean, I was sincere in everything that I said. But I just didn't feel worthy to be there, if that makes sense."

"I would be more concerned if you felt like you were gracing them with your presence. But you don't need to feel like you don't deserve to be there, either. I don't want to compare, but sometimes Miss Lynette could come on pretty strong and be less of a comfort than an irritation. You were born to do what you did today. And you were really good at it. Thank you."

He gathered up his garbage and stood.

She nodded. "Anytime. Please be careful," she said softly, almost hesitantly, like she wasn't sure she had the right to say that.

"I will be. I'm looking forward to that picnic by the river next week."

She smiled. "Me too."

"It's probably going to be a busy week for me, but maybe I'll talk to you some? At any rate, don't get yourself kicked by any horses. Be careful."

"I will be."

It was tempting to walk to her and put his arms around her, and he wanted to kiss her. But he didn't want to rush, didn't want to make her feel like kissing wasn't something he wanted to put a lot of time and effort in. Because he did. Plus, he wasn't exactly sure how she felt about him. Although, she had to feel something. She wouldn't have spent the day the way she'd spent it, if she didn't have some kind of feelings for him.

"I'll call you with any updates."

"Thank you."

He nodded, tightening his fingers around the key in his pocket so he wouldn't be tempted to reach for her instead of walking out the door.

Chapter 12

"I packed a little something for you guys to take on your picnic." Mrs. Hudson lifted two large bags out of the refrigerator in her big country kitchen. "It's a beautiful day for a picnic, and I enjoyed putting everything together."

Blair stood in the kitchen, her eyes wide. It looked like Mrs. Hudson had packed enough food to feed the entire town. "Thank you so much. I never even thought to ask Deacon if I should bring anything."

Mrs. Hudson's face wreathed into a smile, the familiar lines folding up into wrinkles like they were used to being in that shape. "It sounded to me like you guys had a tough week last week, with the car accident and the hospital visits, and you starting a new job, and Deacon doing a funeral." Her voice lowered, infused with sadness. "A hard funeral. Losing a child is never easy. I told Deacon I would take care of it, because I wanted to take all the pressure off you two. You guys deserve a little break."

"My week went really well, but I know Deacon's was hard. I thought his message in church was excellent today, though."

Mrs. Hudson nodded. "He was born to fill a pulpit. He's always had a way of putting things exactly the way we need to hear them. But not too hard and not too much." She kind of shook herself and put a hand on the counter. "I hope you don't mind that all the kids are going with you."

"No. Not at all. I think it'll be fun. I always wanted to have a lot of brothers and sisters." That was the truth. She was looking forward to taking the kids and watching them play.

Mrs. Hudson seemed like such a sweet, easygoing woman. It was hard to imagine her bringing up six boys, but maybe that helped develop her sweetness and sense of humor.

"Hey, Mom. I'm going to dig up some food." One of Deacon's brothers, she was pretty sure it was Zane, walked into the kitchen and headed straight toward the fridge. "Hey, Blair," he tossed over his shoulder at her as he walked by.

"I thought your children were coming today?" Mrs. Hudson said to him, half turning.

"No. Two weeks. Apparently the ex signed them up for summer camp, taking away from my time with them. Made me mad, but I hate to fight with her."

"All four of them?"

"Yeah. I guess she managed to find a camp that would take them all." He grabbed a container of milk and a package of meat and cheese out of the refrigerator before shutting the door. Zane seemed like the most serious of all the brothers, and if she remembered correctly from the gossip that she picked up in the weeks that she'd been in Cowboy Crossing, he had four children. And an ex-wife who enjoyed mind games.

Blair didn't have any more information than that, and she figured with that kind of description, she didn't want to know. Although, she was curious about Deacon's family.

Zane set his things on the counter while Clark and his wife Marlowe walked in. They were bantering back and forth, having some kind of argument about who was more dangerous, which seemed like an odd thing to argue about, but from what Blair had seen of Clark and Marlowe since she'd arrived back in Cowboy Crossing, they were always goofing off together. It was pretty obvious they were in love as well.

Chandler and his fiancée, Ivory, walked in the kitchen, both saying hi to Blair, and they started talking to Zane about the corn crop and planting a cover crop in the oats fields.

"Is Loyal coming?" Chandler asked, looking at his brothers.

Zane's lip pulled back and he shook his head slowly. "You know he hardly ever does."

"I just thought he was maybe pulling out of it since he'd planted that hemp and seemed to hit a goldmine." Chandler grabbed a grape and popped it into his mouth.

Zane shrugged. "All the money in the world can't give him back what he lost."

"Loyal needs a good woman." Marlowe pushed in, comfortable like she was with brothers, and grabbed some grapes for herself.

Clark snorted. "That'd be something I'd like to see – the woman who was brave enough to stay in his presence for more than five seconds. He drives them away."

"He managed to have a kid," Chandler pointed out in a reasonable tone.

"That was before, and you know it. Everything was different then." Zane turned away, but not before Blair saw the pain on his face. Hurt for his brother, she assumed, although she didn't really know what that meant.

Blair started to wonder if Deacon had gotten lost, since all he was doing was changing his clothes in one of the empty upstairs bedrooms. Her gaze kept flicking to the kitchen door, but she didn't miss the sweet smile and even sweet kiss that Chandler and Ivory shared.

Blair got the feeling that they'd had some picnics of their own at the creek and some fun times there.

It was all kind of crazy in the kitchen; she definitely wasn't used to it, although having a big family seemed like a lot of fun

Again, her heart ached for what might have been.

She'd caught some glimpses of Tinsley at church, but she hadn't gotten a chance to talk to her, and she'd been both dreading and looking forward to this all week. Dreading, because she already loved her daughter, but she didn't want to fall in love with her daughter and not be able to leave her.

Being with Tinsley was a two-edged sword. Hot and cold. Seeing Deacon with Tinsley underscored the fact that she made the right choice. Deacon seemed to be happy with the way things were.

She'd almost come to the conclusion that he wouldn't even care if she told him that she was Tinsley's mother. He wouldn't be upset with her for what she'd done.

But she didn't want to mess everything up for him.

Guilt pinched her. Maybe if she hadn't come, Deacon would have paid more attention to Inez, and they would have ended up together. Then Tinsley would have a big family to play in.

She wasn't sure if that were true or not, and she hated to think that it was. It was easier to not think about it.

All those thoughts aside, she couldn't keep the excitement from bouncing like a rubber ball in her chest—she would be spending the afternoon with her daughter for the first time in her life.

The kitchen erupted with laughter when Clark kissed Marlowe and declared himself the winner of their argument since she hadn't been able to respond.

Deacon walked in as the laughter was settling down. Blair thought it interesting the way all the brothers seemed to give deference to Deacon, even though he wasn't the oldest. There was just a respect there, one she was sure he had earned, and even though they laughed and joked with him, he was treated a little different.

"That's cheating, Clark," Deacon said, as he walked straight to Blair. She tried not to look as shocked as she felt when he put his arm around her and faced his brothers. "If you can't let her speak for herself, you can hardly declare yourself the winner."

His hand rested on her shoulder, and although his body didn't touch hers, she could feel his heat. She definitely liked it.

"Okay. Maybe she won the argument, but I won the war, because I got a kiss from my wife, the *least dangerous* person in the room."

Marlowe gasped in mock outrage. "I'm not the least dangerous person..."

And they started bantering back and forth. Again. Blair couldn't watch them and not smile.

Deacon leaned down. "Are you ready to go? We'll leave the zoo behind."

She looked up, laughing. "Is that what this is called?"

"On a good day. Sometimes it degenerates into something more closely resembling a riot." He grabbed the bags from the counter. "Thanks, Mom."

Mrs. Hudson gave him a worried glance, then her expression softened and her eyes landed on Blair. "I hope you two have a good time. I'm sure the kids are already outside, and they've probably run halfway down to the creek. They know not to get in until you get there."

"All right. We'll see you in a bit."

"If you want, you can send the kids up in an hour or so, and I'll get them some ice cream, and we'll play some board games before church."

Blair wasn't sure, but she thought that might have been Mrs. Hudson's way of giving them a little privacy. Odd. She wouldn't have thought Mrs. Hudson would be...trying to set her up with Deacon?

If she didn't know better, that's what she'd say. The idea couldn't hold water though. Surely not.

They walked out of the house to the sound of good-natured laughter.

The kids were long gone. They couldn't even see them.

"As long as all of them stick together, they're allowed to go down to the creek. But they've been around enough that they know they can't leave anyone behind." Deacon put the bags in one hand and casually took hers with his other. Their fingers slid together and clasped, and Blair forgot to breathe.

She felt like something surreal was happening to her—she was walking down through the Hudsons' yard, holding Deacon's hand, getting ready to go on a picnic with him and watch her daughter play for the first time in her life. She couldn't even believe all the things that were happening.

They crossed the driveway and were headed down through the next field when Deacon spoke again. "You're awfully quiet."

Feeling his hand holding hers, just having him beside her, seeing the wide-open spaces that were so different than the prison she'd spent three years in, and the fact that she got her life turned around, nurturing a good relationship with her mother, and a job that could turn out to be the most steady and the best job she'd ever had.

Of all of those things, her daughter and Deacon were the two that she cherished the most.

"I'm savoring."

He snorted. "Savoring? The beautiful day?"

"I suppose that's the least of what I'm savoring, but yes. That." She paused for a minute, unsure about her next words, but he was the one who'd taken her hand. It must mean something to him. "And you. Just being with you." She almost mentioned Tinsley but stopped before she said something that could ruin everything. She didn't want to be too transparent.

"Well, that's an honor. I don't think I've ever had anyone tell me they were savoring me before." There was a little smile in his voice, but there was also a look that made her shiver clear down to her toes. She was pretty sure that wasn't a look that he gave anyone else.

"Well, glad I can be a new experience for you," she said a little flippantly.

"Honestly, Blair. You're a totally new experience for me. I don't know that this is something we want to talk about today, but I've definitely never felt like this before." He squeezed her hand, and she looked up at him. He met her gaze. "I'm serious about you. I don't want to pressure you into anything, but I'm really hoping you feel the same."

Her eyes widened, and her heart seemed to burn as it beat faster and faster. This was what she wanted. What she craved.

But he could lose everything, if the church people didn't accept her.

The thought concerned her, but she just wanted to enjoy being with him. Being special to him.

"Let's just enjoy today. I've never been on a picnic by the creek before."

There was no mistaking the slight drooping of his lips and the disappointment that spread across his face. He'd been hoping for a little more from her, and she wanted to give it to him. But she couldn't. She didn't want to say things and then end up having to leave.

The idea that maybe she could stay had been growing. If Mrs. Hudson accepted her, and if Pastor Wyatt and Lynette accepted her, then maybe there was hope after all.

As they drew closer to the creek, she could hear the gurgle of the water and the chatter of the children laughing and yelling.

"I know Tinsley. And then I saw two other girls and Huck at the house." She thought talking about the children might be a good subject. It seemed to be, because she could feel him relax beside her.

"Huck is Clark's son. And Kylie is Marlowe's daughter. Actually, Kylie is Marlowe's sister's daughter, but when Marlowe's sister and her husband were killed in a car accident, Marlowe adopted her. Then there is RaeAnne, who belongs to my brother Chandler."

"And you're going to marry Chandler and Ivory in a few weeks, right?"

"Yeah." She saw the grin on his face and knew it was something he was proud of.

"It must be an honor for your brother to ask you to marry them."

"It was."

They came around the bend and were able to see the children playing in the grassy area beside the bend in the creek. Blair picked Tinsley out easily and watched her laughing and playing with the others. She wished, with all her heart, that she could be a real mother. But, she told herself, she loved Tinsley enough to let her go.

Chapter 13

Deacon held Blair's hand in his as they walked to the creek. He tried to get some thoughts together to ask the Lord what exactly he should say and what she wasn't ready to hear yet.

And what he was jumping the gun about.

He knew he needed to be careful, because if God ever gave him his dream of being a pastor, whoever he married would end up being a pastor's wife with all the responsibilities that entailed. He needed to make sure he was finding someone who was capable of those things.

Blair was capable. He wasn't sure if she wanted to.

Any time he tried to get close to her, she seemed to pull back and put distance between them. He wasn't sure exactly why.

Maybe they could get to the bottom of it today.

Tinsley, her pigtails bouncing, came running over and grabbed him around the waist. "Daddy! I'm so glad you're here. Can we get in the creek now?"

"Hold on a minute, baby." He put his hand on her head and smoothed her hair down. Someday she'd be grown, she'd no longer call him "Daddy" and wrap her arms around his waist, and he appreciated this. "I don't think you've met Miss Blair. Blair, this is my daughter, Tinsley."

Tinsley lifted her head out from where it was buried in his stomach. "Nice to meet you, Miss Blair."

Just the way she'd been taught.

He didn't expect Blair to have a problem communicating with Tinsley. Blair had been excellent with the children at church, and he did have several parents come to him and tell him so. Of course, he'd had complaints as well—but not about how she treated them.

He hoped, as Blair continued to come to church, continued to live in the town, and continued to show by her life what she was, that those complaints would die down.

It would always be in her past, but it didn't have to be in her present or affect her future.

Blair surprised him. She stared at Tinsley like she'd never seen a child before. She didn't have a cute word to say or a smile. Her mouth kind of hung open, and her eyes searched over Tinsley like she was looking for a gang tattoo.

"Are you okay, Blair?" Deacon finally asked.

Her head shook, and her body twisted like she had just realized that she'd been staring and not very kindly.

"I'm sorry. Tinsley." She cleared her throat. "What a lovely name. It's so nice to meet you." Blair smiled, and Tinsley grinned back at her, but Deacon could tell that Blair's smile seemed forced and strained.

She'd always had some kind of odd reaction when she was around his daughter.

Lord? I can't marry a woman who doesn't love my daughter as much as I do.

He had to still the racing heart and the eagerness of everything in him to be with Blair, if she wouldn't accept Tinsley.

"I've never swum in the creek before. It looks like a lot of fun." Blair's smile had relaxed into something more natural.

"Oh, it is. We hunt for crayfish, and we build dams, and we try to balance on the rocks, and sometimes we try to build a waterfall."

That was just like Tinsley to say a million things in one sentence.

"That sounds like a lot of fun. Maybe I can do it some today."

Relieved that Blair seemed to have recovered from whatever problem she'd had, he said, "Let's eat first. That way when we get cold in the creek, we can walk home."

"Aww. Do we have to? I really wanted to get in the creek right now."

The other kids who were standing behind Tinsley chorused their agreement with her.

"It won't take any time at all. We'll just see what Grandma packed and eat what we want. Aren't you guys hungry?"

"Yeah. I'm always hungry," Huck said, with a hand in the pocket of his shorts. "I hope she made tuna salad. That's my favorite."

"I don't know. We'll have to see."

"Grandma gave me the blanket to carry. It's over there." RaeAnne pointed to a bundle on the grass. She had grown up with her mother, an actress, and acted with more reserve than the other kids.

"How about I spread that out then?" Blair looked up at him, as if asking for permission.

"That sounds great." He held up the bags. "I'll just hold the food."

"Should we trust him with that, guys?" Blair asked the kids surrounding her.

A chorus of noes rang out.

Blair laughed and gave him a look. "Then we better get that blanket spread out pretty fast. Come on."

Her hand slipped out of his as she walked over to the blanket with the children surrounding her, chattering.

Her laughter touched his heart, made it swell. Tinsley walked beside her on her right, and it seemed odd, but her hand seemed to just float over Tinsley's head and down her back. There, but from what he could tell, not quite touching.

Like the invisible touch of a mother's loving hand.

Odd.

He followed them over more slowly, watching as they giggled and covered themselves with the blanket first before everyone grabbed a corner and stretched it out while Blair directed them to slowly lay it down.

"Okay. That's perfect." She put her hands on her hips and turned toward him. "Don't you think so, Deacon?"

He wasn't looking at the blanket. Blair stood with her hands on her hips, her head tilted, the breeze lifting her hair away from her rosy cheeks.

Her lips were pulled back in a smile, and he found himself unable to pull his eyes away. She was beautiful and strong and tough, but she stood beside him in the hospital, being compassionate and caring, and supported him in a way that he hadn't even known he needed but craved.

Deep in his soul, she felt like his perfect match.

But maybe that wasn't the way he was for her. After all, he hadn't supported her through anything. She had no reason to have any feelings for him.

Although she'd allowed him to hold her hand.

"It's perfect," he finally said. He hadn't even looked at the blanket, because he wasn't talking about that. He was talking about whatever was between Blair and himself. He felt like it was perfect. He could only hope she felt the same.

He held up the bags. "Should we get this out and see what Grandma sent?"

The kids all yelled and jumped.

"Everybody find a spot on the blanket."

He got the food out and spread it around, and they prayed over it. Blair bowed her head and whispered an amen after his. He met her eyes as they lifted their heads.

He hoped she wasn't too set on playing in the creek, because he thought he might get to talk to her while the kids were playing.

He felt a little sad about a childhood that hadn't had that kind of fun in it.

He watched as she chatted with the children, asking them about what they were going to do this summer and listening to them as they said how they couldn't wait for their other cousins to come.

"They're talking about Zane's kids," he said low, under the chatter.

She lifted her brows and nodded.

There were other cousins too, since all five of his brothers had children.

Funny, that he was really the only one who didn't, but he had still ended up with a child too.

He had never asked around, and he didn't really know what the townspeople thought about Tinsley, whether they still believed that she was his truly or not. Not that it mattered.

She was his in every way that counted.

The kids all wolfed down their half sandwiches while chattering, mostly with their mouths full. Deacon let it go. It was a picnic, after all.

They also ate their oatmeal raisin cookies and guzzled some water. RaeAnne wasn't quite done when the other ones had finished up.

"Can we go now?" Huck asked with a definite pleading tone in his voice.

"Just hold on. Wait for everyone," Deacon said easily. He'd stretched out on his side, leaning on his elbow. Tinsley was near his head, with Blair on the other side.

Three minutes later, RaeAnne said, "I'm done. May we go now, please?"

"Sure can. Put your garbage in the bag." He held the bag open as the kids gathered up their empty containers and stuck them in the bag before running off.

The kids scattered up and down the creek, and although they could hear the splashing and the music the creek made as it went over the rocks and the yelling of the kids, it was a lot quieter. Not uncomfortable though. Not to him.

"I heard you say you wanted to go play in the creek." He stuck the last of his sandwich in his mouth.

"I think it will be fun. I've never done it before."

"It is fun. I wanted to talk to you some though, sometime."

"Now is fine," she said with a little shrug. "I hardly think I'll last as long as the kids do. I'll probably get cold."

"Yeah. That'll be when we're done. When they start to shiver. Otherwise, I think they'd play all day."

"It makes for a fun childhood."

"Sure does." He straightened up, putting his garbage in the bag and tidying up the blanket. "Would you like to walk a little?"

"Sure."

They stood up, and he held out his hand this time, giving her a choice as to whether or not she wanted to take it. Her eyes went to his before her fingers slid in his palm, and they curled together.

"I'm probably reading more into that than I should be. But I like it."

"I don't know what you're reading into it, but it definitely means I like you."

"Good. Because I really like you." That's not what he wanted to say at all. Wasn't even something he had planned to talk about. But it was the absolute truth.

They went a little ways down the creek, not going far away from the children. The creek was shallow, and they would all be fine, but he wouldn't walk away from them.

"You know it was just my mom and me growing up, and she had to work. So I didn't get to do a lot of things like this. But I always swore if I had children, I would make sure that this was the kind of life they had."

He swung their hands a bit. "I think we all want our kids to have a better life than we did. Isn't that natural? Sometimes we do so much trying to make their lives better that we ruin them, I think. The word spoiled actually applies." He'd seen it over and over in his years as a pastor. "Parents giving their kids everything, and the kids being worthless in return."

"That's true. If we don't have to work for anything, we never develop character."

"Hard times do it too."

"True."

"Where was your dad?" He paused. "Or is that prying?"

"No. You can ask." Her hand twitched in his, and he thought maybe it wasn't her favorite thing to talk about. "I don't know. You know he left my mom for someone else. I heard from him sporadically through my childhood, but it tapered off in high school, and I haven't heard from him since I went to prison." She brushed a hand down her leg. "That would make any relationship awkward. And I guess it was enough to break ours."

"Have you thought about looking him up?"

She shook her head, kicking the ground with her foot. "No. We never had much of a relationship, and I don't want the drama. I guess in my mind it would be nice to have a dad who loves me, but I know the reality isn't going to pan out. I don't want to go through it." She pulled back and lifted her eyes. "Does that make me a bad person?"

He pressed his lips together and shook his head. "No. It just makes you human."

She dropped her eyes and looked away, her eyes tracking the meanderings of the creek as it twisted and turned through the field. "Maybe someday I'll feel strong enough to handle it. But I know he doesn't really want to hear from me anyway. He never has. And to think anything else is just deluding myself. I know that's negative thinking, but positive thinking in this case would just be pie in the sky."

"You're just protecting yourself from being hurt more. He already hurt you enough, with the rejection throughout your childhood and the complete cut of communication. I don't blame you." His heart cried for her, and he tugged on her hand, pulling her to face him. "It's okay to not want to be hurt by people."

She took a deep breath through her nose. "I guess I never really thought about it like that. But you're right. Drama usually hurts, right?"

"Most of the time."

"I promised to tell you why I went to prison."

"You don't have to. Not right now. This isn't supposed to be Blair-confesses-everything day. It's too pretty and nice out for that."

She looked off into the distance and blinked. "No. It's not really hard for me to tell. Just words. It's hard for me to admit to it and to see what the information does to other people when I tell it."

"It's not going to change anything for me," Deacon said with assurance, because he knew it to be true.

Her smile told him that she believed him. He liked that.

"I was in with the wrong crowd. You knew that." Her eyes slid to his, then away. "I'd gotten booked for a couple of things. DUIs. A shoplifting charge." She shrugged, one slim shoulder going up like it didn't matter, but her face said different. "I had a record. I let the people I was with influence me and shut the adults who cared out of my life. There were drugs, of course. One of my friends at the time needed money, and he had the idea to rob a convenience store. I didn't steal anything, but I'd held one of his guns. And that's what got me the time."

She looked like she might say more, then her lips pressed together, and she shoved her hand in her pocket.

He squeezed the hand he was holding, and she squeezed back, but she didn't look at him.

She'd trusted him with so much—first her dad and now her prison sentence. He wasn't sure whether to push or not, but he figured he'd ask the question, then leave it up to her as to whether or not she would answer.

He took a breath and said with soft, measured words, "I heard there was a baby."

There, he said it. The thing that most bothered him about everything.

"There was." She swallowed tightly. "That's probably the most painful thing out of any of it."

Yeah, that was all he needed to hear. He thought about all the things he counseled with other women over the years, women who were eaten up with guilt, who believed the lie that it was a part of their body or just tissue.

Women who had finally seen an ultrasound and realized what they had been duped into doing. It wasn't an act that was ever going to leave. When a person killed her own child, they lived with that for the rest of their lives.

He'd seen it.

He didn't want to give empty words to Blair. Most of all because she hadn't asked for any.

After a long time of staring at the ground, she finally said, "You know, when you're a teenager, and your life is stretched out ahead of you, and you're so excited about everything, and then things don't work out the way you think they should. You realize the people in your life that you resented the most because they didn't tell you what you wanted to hear were actually the ones that loved you the most. And they were right. Then you wish that you could go back and you could do it again, and you could just listen and do what they wanted you to, without having to experience the pain on your own. Because it wasn't just you that hurt that whole time. The people who loved you went through it too, and what you did hurt them every bit as much as it hurt you. Maybe even more."

She shook her head, her face drawn. "Why was I so stupid?" Her eyes searched his. "What made you so smart? How did you know? How did you know not to do the things that I did? Why was I the stupid one? Why didn't I listen to my mom? All those questions, and they're pointless now. It's done and over with, and the only way through it is forward."

He wanted to put his arms around her and comfort her, but she was frustrated and upset, and he wasn't sure his touch was welcome. He didn't want to go there. Not now.

But he put a hand on her shoulder, because there was something necessary and elemental in the touch of one human to another. "I can't answer those questions. I was never tempted to run with a bad crowd. I just wasn't. I don't know why. It wasn't anything good that I had done. I don't know if it was God protecting me or my mom's prayers. Or whether God just ordained it that way. I don't know. All I know is that I'm never going to understand everything about God, because there's too much. Any being who can do what He did is beyond my comprehension. That's where the childlike trust comes in. Because that's all I can do—just trust."

Blair's sigh was a whisper, almost taken away by the wind. And then, slowly, she took a slight step closer and put a hand lightly on his chest. Her head tilted up, her eyes on his chin.

"Is this okay?" she asked softly.

He wasn't sure exactly what she was asking. "Yes." The answer came off his tongue, even without knowing the question. Easily.

His chest ached where her hand rested, and he wanted her to press harder, wanted her to step closer. But he didn't want to push her, and he didn't want to take advantage of her vulnerability right now.

From the counseling that he'd done, he knew one of the deepest hurts a person could experience was the rejection, or the neglect, of their parents. It was hard and left scars for the rest of their life. Blair would have that. And he wanted to help heal her, but the privilege wasn't his. Not right now.

Her eyebrows twitched, and she bit her lip. "And if I step closer?"

His breath trembled as he let it out. "That's fine too." His words came out soft but rough. It was hard to speak when all he wanted to do was feel.

His hands hung at his sides. He fought the urge to lift them up and put them around her, waiting. He wasn't sure exactly what he was waiting for. Waiting for her to be ready.

"Why does being with you always make me feel like I can be better?" she asked softly, still staring at his chin.

He wasn't sure exactly what she meant and what that had to do with her position, and so he didn't answer.

"Maybe the way a tree casts shade and a person is drawn to the coolness...you just seem to have so much integrity and honesty. I guess I see that and I want it for me too."

Disappointment spiraled in his stomach. That wasn't what he wanted from her. It was the way he wanted to live, true, and he was glad she saw it. But from Blair, of all people, he'd wanted more.

He stood still, throat too tight for words, heart too full to figure out what he wanted to say anyway.

She pressed her lips together before she whispered so softly he almost didn't hear, "But there's an attraction too. I'm sorry. I know that's probably not what you want. But I fight it every time I'm close to you."

He closed his eyes, breathing out slowly. That's what he wanted. That's what he'd been waiting for. His hands came up and settled on her back, and he pulled her closer.

"Me too," he said, his cheek down on the top of her head. "Me too."

He could watch the children from where his head was on hers, and hear their laughter and their splashing, and knew that everything was okay with them. But it was hard to focus, with the writhing of his heart, and the scattering of his thoughts, and the way he just wanted to move closer and be like that forever. Maybe that made him crazy.

Chapter 14

Blair had known Deacon was different. It was one of the things that was so attractive about him. Different than all the guys she'd known. Being with him made her different too.

She loved that about him. That she wasn't fighting to keep herself up against the tidal wave trying to pull her down. Rather, she was fighting to make herself better, not necessarily to deserve him, but because he inspired that in her.

She supposed this was what all the teachings from her childhood had meant about surrounding herself with the right kind of friends. Deacon was definitely the right kind of friend. She wasn't feeling friendly toward him. Or, maybe more accurately, she didn't want to be just friends with him.

She wasn't sure exactly how he felt, but she appreciated the fact that he wasn't pushing her to do more than what she was ready for.

Although, the way she felt, she was ready to do more than what they were doing.

Holding him close gave her strength in a way she hadn't anticipated, though. It didn't take away those feelings of rejection and the questions of why hadn't she been good enough for her dad to love her. But just having him there, understanding and offering his support, was better than anything else in her life so far.

Maybe she was taking advantage of him, since he seemed so hesitant to hold her. Maybe they could talk about that, in a bit, after she was ready to let go.

"Uncle Deacon! Miss Blair!" Huck's shrill voice shot across the creek and meadow. "Are you guys coming? We want to go down to the deep part where the tree is and see if we can walk across."

Deacon's voice came low and soft. "You ready? Do you want to go?"

She nodded, leaning back just a little. "Thank you."

He looked down, and their eyes met. He was shaking his head. "No. Thank you, for trusting me."

She took a breath. Because that's what it was. She trusted him. Completely. Maybe she shouldn't. Although, there was just something about him that went along with his integrity and the strength that he exuded. Maybe it was fanciful, but she kinda felt that someone who walked so close to Jesus couldn't help but shine a little bit like Him. Maybe that was it.

It made her feel like she wasn't good enough. Not good enough to be here, not good enough to be held. Not good enough to be with him.

"Thank you for being the kind of man that I can trust." She forced her lips up into a smile, one she hoped looked genuine. "Now, I get to have the childhood thrill of wading in the creek."

He smiled along with her, even if he wasn't completely fooled by her forced attempt. In her experience, when she forced it, the true feelings eventually came along.

"Well, I think this is a little different. When they walk on the log across the creek, the goal is to not fall in." He winked at her. "It's pretty deep down here. They're not allowed to go unless I'm right with them."

"Oh, sounds dangerous."

"It's not. They don't have to swim, and there's no danger with current or anything. They're just pretty young yet."

This time, she didn't wait for him to offer his hand but took it with hers. He looked over with a smile, and she assumed that meant he liked it.

Man, she couldn't figure it out. Maybe she just wasn't used to moving that slow. She'd never been with a man who had not let her know with leering looks if not actual words exactly what he wanted. This was new. Respectful, and she liked it.

"Daddy, remember last time I was able to walk the whole way across?" Tinsley called from where she stood at the edge of the creek where it began to widen and deepen.

Now that they were closer, Blair could see the log that stretched across the stream. Just an old tree that had fallen down and spanned the creek.

"I remember, baby. Bet you can do it again too."

Tinsley gave a huge smile, and Blair's heart twisted. She was so beautiful. And happy.

That little nagging voice reminded her that she was keeping something from Deacon, something important. Not just about who Tinsley's mother was. But who the father was too.

"All right, guys, if you all make it across without falling in, I'll walk across too," Deacon called, the smile evident in his voice.

"Yay!" the kids all called as they ran to the edge of the tree and climbed on. Huck started over first, and he fell in about four steps later. All the kids laughed, and Blair had to as well, just because his face looked so surprised as his arms windmilled before he tipped into the water.

He popped back up, grinning, and after the noise died down, Deacon said, "A little slower, buddy. You could make it, but you gotta go slow and steady."

"But when I go fast, I get through it quicker."

"Do it your way then. Or you can do it like last time when you tried my way. You made it across then."

"Uncle Deacon said it was like life, Huck. Slow and steady." RaeAnne, on the log next, said that over her shoulder as she walked across the log, slow and steady. Unlike the rest of the children, her hair wasn't wet. She'd been in the creek, but not with as much abandon.

"That's right, RaeAnne. I'm impressed that you remembered. It's actually a good life lesson," Deacon said casually. He wasn't preaching at the kids. Blair figured they wouldn't remember anyway if he did. It was less about what he said and more about what he did.

Maybe if she'd had a good example growing up, she wouldn't have needed to worry about following what her mom said, and she could have just watched and followed that good example.

Flawed logic, because her mom had been a good example. Maybe she was just so resentful that her dad didn't care and wasn't around. Maybe that was the problem.

Shoving those thoughts aside, she tried to focus on the here and now. Thinking about that stuff never helped.

RaeAnne made it across, and the other kids cheered for her. She turned around. "Kylie, come on. You can do it."

Blair found it sweet that RaeAnne was encouraging rather than taunting.

Kylie stepped up to the log, a little timid and unsure.

Behind her, Tinsley said, "You can do it, Kylie. Just go slow."

Kylie made it a little further than Huck did, and then she fell in with a squeal and a laugh.

Beside her, Deacon watched intently until her head popped up from the water, her face decked out in a mile-wide grin.

"I think it's just as fun to fall in as it is to get across," she said as she climbed back out onto the side where she came from.

Tinsley was next, and Blair's heart trembled in her chest. Was this what it was like to worry about a child?

She'd thought about her baby, her little girl, every day of her life. In the last three years, she'd even been praying for her, which wasn't necessarily something she'd done in prison too much. Once she'd started to get her life straightened out, she'd done more praying.

Tinsley started across, taking one slow careful step and then another, her arms stretched out and her face smiling, although her brows were drawn together in concentration.

Deacon leaned down. "I'm going to assume that you're not squeezing my hand in a death grip because you've all of a sudden decided that you're madly in love with me."

She gasped. She hadn't even realized she'd been doing it. Her fingers loosened immediately. "I'm so sorry. I didn't know. Are you okay?"

He laughed. "Of course I'm okay. I was worried about you."

Tinsley took another step, wobbling some. Blair couldn't take her eyes off her, and she couldn't stop her little catch of breath until Tinsley caught her balance.

Deacon's gaze shifted from Blair to Tinsley and back again. She could see the movement of his head out of the corner of her eye, but she just couldn't bring herself to look at him. Couldn't bring herself to take her eyes off Tinsley.

"You know if she falls, she'll be okay. You saw the other two. They're fine."

She closed her eyes. "I know." Her breath came out like it was going over potholes. Her eyes opened back up immediately. She needed to see.

Tinsley took another careful step.

"I don't know what the problem is." Actually, she shouldn't have said it, because she did know what the problem was.

She should fix it. This would be a good time to tell him. Except, no, it wouldn't. Because she needed to see if Tinsley was going to make it across or not.

Her heart beat fast.

"Maybe you should go next, so you can see this is not a big deal."

"I'll go. I just..." She was just nervous about her child. She hadn't had years to get used to seeing her do dangerous things. Or even nondangerous things that felt dangerous to a mother's heart.

"Will it make you feel better if I go over and walk behind her?"

She shook her head. "No. I can see how this helps the kids. They're doing something that seems dangerous but probably isn't going to hurt them, and it helps them see that they can do hard things. I get that, and this is really great for them. It's just...scary."

"Did you just figure that out when Tinsley got on? I didn't notice you squeezing my fingers with the other ones."

"Maybe. Maybe Tinsley just seems different." There. That was the truth. She needed to be honest. Tinsley was halfway across, and Blair tried to force herself to relax. "Looks like she's going to make it."

"She's made it before. She's actually a pretty smart kid, and that's part of it, having control of your brain and your emotions, so you don't get psyched out. It really is good for them."

"I guess in a weird way you're saying that maybe I'm trying to be too careful with the kids?"

"Maybe. It's never easy to see someone get hurt. That can happen. But the goal of life isn't to not get hurt."

"Yeah. I guess there's a balance there." They shared a smile at her play on the word balance.

"Funny, but true. You can't let them do stupid things, but you can't keep them from doing all the things that could be good for them and help them to grow. You know, we could just let them sit inside and watch TV and play video games all day. And I suppose if we did that, they'd learn all the cultural norms of the rest of kids in the country. And maybe in today's day and age, that's more important than actually knowing how to take care of yourself and knowing how far to push so you can push yourself to be better."

"She's almost over." Blair put a hand on her heart and exhaled sharply.

"I think this was harder on you than it was on anyone else."

"I think so." She laughed a nervous laugh,

"Huck's gonna want to try to make it across again, then you and I get a turn." He tugged her hand, and she followed him down the bank to the edge of the creek.

Huck was already on the log, and this time he was going slow, with his hands out and placing his feet carefully. The log was big enough that there was plenty of room for his feet. It wasn't that high from the water either.

So it wasn't scary. There was just something about knowing you didn't want to get wet.

Huck made it across, and everybody cheered.

"Uncle Deacon! Are you coming?" Kylie hollered.

"Yeah, Daddy! Your turn!"

"Do you want to go first?" Deacon said in Blair's ear.

"No. You go ahead. Show me how it's done." Being this close to the water and the log and seeing the narrowness she'd have to walk on made her more nervous than she thought she would be. She watched as he crossed with surprising ease. "Is the water cold?"

Deacon snorted. "Maybe you ought to touch it. Stick your fingers in and check it out. Because, you know, if you haven't done it before, it might take a little practice before you can actually make it all the way across."

"Really?" She slanted her gaze at him. "I think you're saying you don't think I can make it across?"

"Hey, don't put words in my mouth. I didn't say that."

"I think you did, Uncle Deacon." RaeAnne tilted her head and tapped her chin, which made Blair smile, because it was obvious she was imitating one of the adults in her life.

The other girls called out, "You did!"

Deacon put his hands on his hips and mock glared at RaeAnne. "Really? Are you ladies all going to gang up on me?"

"Hey, the girls have to stick together. You're bigger and stronger, but we have strength in numbers."

"How about that, Huck? We're outnumbered? They think they're gonna beat us." Deacon narrowed his eyes. "I think I should go over and toss her in the creek."

All of the children said yes to that, with Huck and Kylie jumping up and down, and Tinsley shouting, "Go do it, Daddy."

"I think all of my teammates left me."

"It's funny how the children just love the Three Stooges type of violence. It gets them every time." Deacon grinned.

"So, if I say, 'how about let's push Uncle Deacon in,' they'll do it?"

The kids all looked at her for about two seconds, and then RaeAnne said, "Hey! That's a great idea. We'll help you." She put her hand on Deacon's back and started to push. All the other kids joined in with Deacon good-naturedly allowing it as he stepped forward a couple of steps.

He put one foot on the log, then another, then held his hand up. "Hold up a second. If I'm going to go in the water, I need to take my boots off."

"No! You're going in with your boots on," Huck called.

RaeAnne said loudly, to be heard over all the other noise, "Wait! Let's let him take them off. Then maybe he'll get in and swim with us some too."

"Will you, Uncle Deacon? Will you swim with us?" Kylie asked.

"Daddy, if you fall in, then you have to swim with us, okay?" Tinsley asked, hope shining in her eyes. Then she leaned toward the other kids and made pushing motions with her hands, like her dad couldn't see it or something. Which of course made Blair laugh.

"Okay, I'll agree to that, but I can't fall in because somebody pushes me, it has to be an honest fall." He set his boots aside, and stood up, lifting his brow and looking at the children. "Agreed?"

They all looked kind of guilty, with Tinsley putting her arms behind her back and rocking back and forth.

"Agreed?" he prompted again.

Huck dug his toes in the ground. "Agreed," he said a little reluctantly.

Deacon lifted another brow at the girls. Waiting.

"Agreed," they said together.

He turned to face Blair, who was having a hard time trying to tear her eyes off his bare feet for some reason.

It wasn't like she hadn't seen a man's bare feet before. Or that she even thought about people's feet. It was just weird, of all the situations she'd ever seen Deacon in over the last few weeks that she'd been here, preaching, and the hospital, even at the diner and with Inez, or at her house, she just hadn't thought about his bare feet.

It made him vulnerable and more human almost.

"Okay, so I'll go back over and get Blair, and get her to walk over with me. If I fall in the water, I'll swim with you guys. Is that a deal?" He looked around at the kids who were grinning and watching and listening.

They chorused a bunch of yeses, and he started across the log again.

After about four steps, he wiggled and tilted way over to his right side, and Blair thought he was going in the water.

"Ouch. Stepped on a briar or something." Deacon took his foot and held it up, balancing on one foot on the log. Blair's fingernails cut into her palms as she watched. She was pretty sure he was going to fall in.

"Oh yeah, I see it." He wobbled and held his hand out, balancing himself. "I don't think I'm going to be able to get it, though. It'll have to wait until later." He put his foot back down carefully.

He started walking again, though his balance was worse, and Blair attributed that to the thorn he had in his foot.

With a couple more wobbles, he made it across, grinning at her. "You ready?"

"Do you want me to take a look at that thorn in your foot first?"

"Nah. Maybe later. It hurts, but it'll be okay. You don't have anything to take it out with anyway, and it wasn't sticking out far enough for me to grab a hold of it with my fingernails."

"Okay. When we get back to the house, we'll do it."

"Are you okay with falling in?"

"So now you think I'm going to fall in?"

"No. I just wanted to make sure you're okay with it. There's always that chance."

"I don't know. It wasn't as scary when we were back on the bank watching the kids. When I'm standing here looking at it, it seems like the very worst thing that could happen would be that I would fall in."

"Tell you what. If you lose your balance and start to fall, I'll go with you."

She narrowed her eyes, looking at him. Pursing her lips, she said, "Does that mean that I have to fall in with you if you start?"

"Pretty sure the unwritten law is people don't let their pastor fall in the creek by himself."

"Well, I haven't been here very long, are you my pastor?"

"Do you have a different one?" He tilted his head.

"Good point." She looked down. She might've gone to a few different churches kinda sporadically over the last few years, but no, she didn't have a pastor.

He touched her chin with his finger. "Hey. There's nothing wrong with that. Chin up."

She closed her eyes, then deliberately opened them and met his. "I know. I don't know why I have to be so serious all the time. I guess I just hate all the things I've done that I can't be proud of."

"Forgive yourself. God's already done it."

She nodded. "It sounds easy. Sometimes reality is just a little harder."

"Sometimes we make it harder. So hard to say, 'here, God, take this.' Then walk away from it. You gotta reach in your mind and take any of those thoughts that need to come out and toss them."

"Another thing that sounds easy."

"It's completely possible though."

"You're speaking from experience?"

"I just know God wouldn't command us to do something that we couldn't. 'Take every thought captive.' We can do it."

She'd forgotten about that verse. It was true; it made sense that God wouldn't command people to do something they couldn't.

She liked the idea of grabbing her thoughts and putting them in prison. "All right, I'm taking captive the thought that I might fall in the water."

"Sounds like you're ready." He stepped off the log and to the side. "You go first. I'll be behind you. I'll even hold your hands if you want."

"Is that cheating?" she asked over her shoulder.

"I don't think so. It's your first time. I think you're allowed to have a little help."

"Okay. If you're sure it can't be considered cheating, I would definitely like that help." She took a breath to steady herself. Her lungs felt like they couldn't get enough air, and her knees were shaking. "I don't know why I'm so nervous about this. It's not like some of the kids haven't fallen in already. It's not that big of a deal."

"It's not, but I understand how it could be scary for you, since you've never been in the creek before." He paused for just a moment. "You do know how to swim, correct?"

"Yes. I had a friend who had summer passes at the pool in Trumbull. I learned there. But I'm not the greatest."

"It's not even over your head. But I just wanted to check."

"Okay, here goes." She put one foot on the log, sticking her arms out. His hands slid down her forearms to her fingers, palms up. He didn't try to grab a hold of her but left that up to her, and she appreciated it.

Her first trembling step was followed by another one and another until they were almost halfway across. "I'm starting to think we're gonna make it."

"I always thought we would."

From over on the other side of the bank, Huck called, "Uncle Deacon, push her in!" All the other kids started calling the same thing, and behind her, Deacon chuckled.

"Bloodthirsty little buggers."

She probably would have been okay, if she hadn't had to laugh at Deacon calling his nieces and nephew bloodthirsty little buggers.

"Oh! Oh, no!" She tilted way over to the side. Deacon's hands steadied her, and she tilted back the other way. Again his hand was there, and she almost had herself balanced and thought she'd be okay, except she saw the water under her, and her reflection in it, and the precarious way they seemed to be perched on the log, and panic grabbed her throat with a cold, dead grip, weakening her knees and curling in her stomach.

She lost her confidence and almost fatalistically started to fall.

"No." Behind her, Deacon breathed the word under his breath. "I don't think I can stop you," was the last thing she heard him saying before she tumbled off the log, and at that point, his hands gripped hers, and they fell together into the water with a big splash.

Chapter 15

The cold water was a shock.

Deacon was able to keep his balance, enough to land on his feet, and he didn't let go of Blair's hands.

She screamed and he grunted, and the water splashed all around them, coming up almost to her chest.

In the back of his mind, he could hear the kids screaming; they loved it. As long as Blair was okay, he didn't consider it a bad thing.

Yeah, she was okay. He could hear laughter. It filled the air and waved out over the water.

He let go of one of her hands, tugging her around. She was still laughing, pushing her hair out of her face which had gotten wet with the splashes, because she hadn't gone under.

"Do it again, Daddy. Do it again!" Tinsley jumped up and down on the far side of the bank.

The other kids were laughing as well. But Deacon was focused on Blair and hardly heard them.

"Are you okay?" That smile and the fact that she was standing right in front of him indicated that she was, but he wanted to make sure.

"Nothing like facing your fears." She laughed.

"I hadn't thought about it quite like that, but that's true. You faced them."

"And I conquered them," she said jauntily, but then she finished pushing her hair back and met his gaze, and neither one of them had anything to say.

One of his hands had somehow landed on her waist under the water, probably to steady her, while the other one still held her hand. Water lapped between them, but only a couple of inches separated them.

Deacon breathed her air, wanting nothing more than to lower his head and do what he'd been thinking about almost from the time he'd laid eyes on her in her mother's doorway.

His heart thumped hard in his chest, and her breath was unsteady. Matching his.

Suddenly his throat was dry, and he couldn't swallow, couldn't talk, and didn't want to.

A splash of cold water broke the spell that had fallen on them, and two more followed closely behind, as first Huck, then Kylie and Tinsley jumped in the water.

RaeAnne still stood on the side of the bank, coming down with a little more decorum.

Deacon never resented the children, but he did kind of wish he had a few more minutes alone with Blair.

The kids swam over and started a splashing contest, and he let go of Blair's hand, and somehow it ended up being boys against girls which was not fair in terms of numbers, but he was the best splasher. He couldn't grow up with five brothers and not be good.

It was at least an hour later before they climbed out of the creek. They hadn't brought towels, and they dripped as they walked back to the picnic area. The kids had their arms around their stomachs and were shivering.

"Here, Tinsley. You can carry this bag." He handed one of the bags to Tinsley, then said, "Huck, you can carry this one."

He grabbed the blanket, picking it up and shaking it, making sure there were no crumbs or bugs left on it. He draped it around Blair's shoulders. She was shivering too, and it was for warmth but also for modesty.

"Thank you." She looked at him with eyes that glowed with happiness, her face completely relaxed. He didn't really know and didn't know how to tell, but he almost thought there was some admiration in her eyes.

He kind of thought, after they fell off the log, that something had shifted between them. He felt it in the water but wasn't sure what kind of name to put on it, or even if it was just his imagination.

"You're welcome," he said, his voice hoarse.

"Do we have to leave?" Tinsley asked.

"Yeah. I think Grandma was going to have some ice cream ready for you guys when we got back. But you need to get dried off and warmed up so we can go to church tonight."

He probably should do some studying, although he did have a sermon ready. It was hard to imagine leaving Blair, but she'd need to go back to her mother's as well. He'd drop her off.

"Will that blanket work until we get to your mom's house?"

"It'll have to. I don't have any spare clothes to put on." She wasn't complaining, and she said it with a smile.

"I can grab some of mine. They'd be too big but would be warmer than your wet things."

"I'd like that." He was pretty sure with the look on her face that she really would.

He put his socks and boots on, and they started up the hill.

This time, Blair's hand slipped into his like it belonged there. And he hoped with all his heart that it did.

He had to limp a little because of the thorn still stuck in his foot. He tried to be inconspicuous about it, because he didn't want to bring a lot of attention to it, but Blair noticed.

The kids were running in front of them when she said in a low voice only he could hear, "That thorn still bothering you?"

"Yeah. I'll take you home first, then I'll try to get it out before I need to head to the church."

"I can work on it, if you have a pair of clippers or something I can use." Her eyes crinkled. "That's if you trust me."

He chuckled. "I think I trust you. You trusted me on the log, and I let you down."

"You didn't let me down. You fell with me just like you said you would. I like and admire a man that keeps his word."

"I hope I always do that. It's something I strive for."

"I've never heard anyone say you haven't. In fact, it's something you're known for. A man of integrity. That's what people say when they talk about you."

She pulled her gaze away and looked across the field at the house coming in sight, her smile fading. It wasn't hard to guess which direction her thoughts had wandered.

"Hey. Stop. Please. Don't go wherever you're going in your head."

"I'm just going to the truth. Because we both know that's not my reputation."

"But you can start today building the reputation that you want."

She didn't say anything but kept on walking. She knew it. And they'd already been through it before. He supposed the words that people had said about her had hurt her, maybe made her feel like she was less than them or that she couldn't ever turn her life around. He didn't know. He just hated it when she looked down.

They walked in silence the rest of the way back to the house, which was much less noisy than it had been when they left. His mom shuffled the kids to the extra clothes that they had packed and sent them to get changed. They were dry enough that they didn't drip through the house.

"You want to sit here at the bar, and I'll grab some clothes and bring them down. I'll change while I'm up there and grab a pair of clippers, if you don't mind looking for that thorn."

"Not at all. Take your time. I'm fine right here."

He started to turn away, but hesitated, and put his hand on her shoulder. "Thanks. I had a really great time. I appreciate you coming and being such a good sport."

"I enjoyed it. Thank you."

He wanted to linger, but he needed to get her home. She'd been away from her mom for a while. She hadn't said anything, but he saw her eyes strayed to the clock in the kitchen on the microwave, and he turned to go. "Be right back."

BLAIR PULLED THE BLANKET tighter around her shoulders. Her lips just wouldn't turn down, and her heart practically glowed in her chest.

She'd spent the afternoon with Tinsley. Got to watch her play and talk to her—play with her. It'd been more than her mother's heart had ever thought she could hope for.

When she'd come back to Cowboy Crossing, she thought she might get to see her daughter once in a while. She'd never thought she'd actually get to spend time with her and watch her play. Talk to her and touch her.

There were only a few things on earth that could be better. She could hear Tinsley call her mom. Or she'd have Tinsley in her house and actually *be* a mom.

But some things were too good to be true.

She was happy with what she had.

Although, being with Deacon almost overshadowed them. The way he looked at her, like he liked her. No. That he more than liked her. The admiration in his eyes, and the way he teased her and held her. Especially the way he held her.

Of course, there was the little voice in her head that said if he really loved her, he would have kissed her.

But he hadn't. Hadn't even made a move to. So maybe it was all just her being forward, and him being polite. Too polite to tell her to back off.

That would be like Deacon. He wouldn't want to hurt anyone's feelings. Of course, she didn't think he normally went around holding people's hands. That had to mean something.

"Are you warm enough, my child?" Mrs. Hudson walked into the kitchen with an arm out. She didn't stop until she had wrapped her arms around Blair and squeezed her tight.

Blair closed her eyes. It felt good to just feel loved and accepted, and that was what Mrs. Hudson's hug did. Made her feel accepted.

"I'm plenty warm, thank you so much," Blair finally said when Mrs. Hudson's arms relaxed around her.

"Deacon will be down in a minute." Her kindly eyes crinkled. She walked around the counter so that she was facing Blair. "From the way the kids were chattering, it sounds like you guys had a really great time in the creek. I'm sorry you got all wet."

"I think that's the point of going swimming in the creek, isn't it?" Blair asked with a smile. "I've never been, and it was more fun that I had imagined. I can see the draw. Especially for a child."

"Yes. They have a way of putting wonder into everything. It's good for us sometimes to try to look through the eyes of a child. Keeps us young." Mrs. Hudson's finger traced the counter slowly. "Could I ask you something?" She hesitated. "You don't have to answer me if you don't want to. There's no offense if you don't."

"Okay?" A sixth sense stirred the hair at the back of her neck, and a cold, wicked wind trickled its fingers across her skin.

"Are you going to tell Deacon that Tinsley is your daughter?"

Mrs. Hudson had taken her by surprise. She couldn't stop the gasp that escaped her lips. No one knew. No one, not even her own mother.

She probably had the deer-in-the-headlights look, where she looked right and left and up and down and anywhere except straight into Mrs. Hudson's gaze. Because she couldn't deny it. Her reaction had already given her away. Was she about to be found out? What was she going to do? What was Deacon going to say?

She decided she just had to go with the truth. "I wasn't going to tell anyone."

"Why not?" Mrs. Hudson asked, sounding reasonable.

"Because I made a choice to give her up. It was the right choice. But I have to live with it." She could have made another choice. It might've been the easier choice at the time, but then she wouldn't have seen Tinsley today, happy and playing.

She couldn't have done it anyway. Just because something was defenseless didn't mean it was worthless. As messed up as she'd always been, she'd always fought for the underdog.

"Of course, that's your decision. I won't say anything."

"How did you know?" she asked, finally trying to figure it all out as it clicked in her brain.

"I didn't. I just had a hunch. You two look very similar to me. But it's the way you look at her. I just thought if I asked, I might be right."

Blair met her wise gaze. She figured raising six boys had infused more than the average amount of wisdom into Mrs. Hudson.

"I know small towns are notorious for gossip, but I really won't say anything. Although I think you might be surprised. I think Deacon should know."

Blair automatically shook her head, denying it. "That will mess everything up. He's got everything figured out now. I didn't do right by him. I was selfish, and I chose the best person for my daughter. But I wasn't considerate of what was best for him." She sighed. "He's made the best of it. It's not right for me to come into his life and mess it up again."

"I don't understand how having you in his life would mess it up."

"Haven't you heard the people at church say that I'm not good enough to teach? What do you think they'd say if they found out I was Tinsley's mother? Deacon would really get caught in the crossfire."

"You could talk to him about it and see what he said. Maybe you wouldn't want people to know. Maybe it wouldn't matter to him. I don't think I raised him to be so concerned about what everybody else thinks. I raised him to think for himself and stand against the current if necessary."

Blair took a shaky breath. She felt like she had bubbles in her lungs. "I'm scared. I'm just...I'm scared of what will happen. I don't want to take that chance." Life had already been so hard. She didn't want to rock the boat on this one. As much as she wanted to be with Tinsley.

Mrs. Hudson's hand came down on top of Blair's which were clasped together in front of her. It was warm and soft and infused calmness into her scattered and racing thoughts.

"The decision is yours. You do what you feel is right. What God wants you to do." She paused for just a moment, as though searching for the right words. "I know that Deacon can be intimidating. Because he's...he's so close to the Lord. So confident in what is right. He seems to choose the right path so easily and be certain of his way." Something that looked like sadness seemed to have entered her eyes, and Blair couldn't have stopped listening now for anything.

"But please don't forget he's human just like the rest of us. And while Jesus *is* close to him, and he does have a special relationship with the Lord, he's still just a man, with all of those weaknesses and with all of those wants and needs. He's not perfect, and he needs someone else who's not perfect to take a risk and stand beside him. Because it's not good that a man should be alone."

Mrs. Hudson straightened slowly and patted Blair's hand again.

She backed off and turned to go toward the sink as Deacon walked in the kitchen. "Hey, Blair. Sorry it took me so long. Mom left me upstairs in charge of getting the kids dressed. We had a small kerfuffle with underwear that disappeared."

He held up the clothes that were in his hand. "I'm sorry you've been sitting here in your wet clothes. I brought you dry ones."

She stood, still pondering Mrs. Hudson's words. She hadn't been putting Deacon on a pedestal or thinking that he was not human. Or was she?

There was no doubt that she saw him as a spiritual giant. And what had Mrs. Hudson said, something about being intimidated?

Maybe she was. She had considered that it was respect, but maybe it was more than that, and maybe she was doing him a disservice.

She wasn't sure exactly, but she stood and smiled a thank you as she took the clothes from Deacon, and he pointed her to the bathroom to change.

"Mom will feed the kids in here. I've got clippers, and I'll be working on my foot in the living room. Then I'll take you home. Okay?"

"If you wait, I'll do it," she offered, as she stood in the doorway.

"I'll wait." His eyes met hers across the room, and she again felt the way she had in the water, only his gaze seemed more intense, and she felt even less able to pull away.

She wanted to close the distance now, and...and she wasn't sure. Doing that could end up hurting Deacon more than she already had. Despite what his mother said, her relationship with him was almost certain to cause him hardship at the church. Almost certain.

She tore her gaze away and walked to the bathroom.

Chapter 16

Deacon sat on the couch, the clippers in his hand, flipping end over end. He wasn't sure whether he could term this the best afternoon of his life, but it was definitely in the top few. He had a lot of good memories with his family and with his daughter, but Blair just fit him in a way that was hard for him to describe.

Is this what a soulmate is, Lord?

He felt like it was. It was odd, because no one would look at Blair and him and think soulmates. But he didn't even need to look at her, he just needed to be near her, and he felt like he was complete in a way that he never had been before.

She made him feel hot and cold, made him tremble, yet made him feel strong at the same time. Like he could slay dragons if she would just stand beside him. Physical dragons. He couldn't touch the mental ones in her head. Only she could. He couldn't change the past for her.

He was encouraged though, because he thought she might be softening toward him. A good thing, since he was falling for her, if he hadn't fallen already. Something about the sappy grin that he couldn't keep off his face when she walked in the room. That would give it away.

She appeared in the doorway, and immediately every part of his body was on alert. Her hair was still wet and hung down each shoulder, and his clothes looked baggy on her. She was beautiful to him. The sparkle in her eyes, the color in her cheeks, the smile on her mouth, and the way she looked at him. Made him feel like he could do anything, and would, if she'd just look at him like that again.

She walked to the couch, and he moved his feet so she could sit down.

She didn't say anything, and he didn't break the silence either, thinking instead how odd it was. Feet were just feet, but not even his mother ever touched his.

She held her hand out, and he set the clippers in it, brushing her hand deliberately and sharing a little smile with her, thinking that maybe the same spark that was shooting up his arm was shooting up hers as well.

"Thank you," she said softly.

"My pleasure," he said, meaning those words absolutely literally. Those sparks were a little prickly, but they were nothing but pleasure.

She took his foot, her hands cool and soft, and he leaned back and closed his eyes.

Lord, is this the woman for me? I sure hope so. Never felt like this before.

"Tell me if I hurt you."

He didn't say anything. She could take a ten-foot crater out of his foot, and he wouldn't say anything as long as she continued to sit and hold it in her lap.

He lay there, just enjoying the feel of her fingers gently working on his foot, and he didn't move when the pinch of the clippers bit into the sensitive skin on his arch.

Not nearly long enough later, she said, "All right. I got it. It wasn't very big. Sometimes those little ones are the worst."

"Thank you." He didn't want to move, wanted to lie right there, even for the rest of his life. But he lifted his head up. "I know you need to check on your mom. Thanks for being patient."

"It's been my pleasure." She slanted him a glance while her fingers lightly ran over the soft skin of the top of his foot. "Thanks so much for a wonderful afternoon. I'm sorry you have to take me home. You probably could use a nap. I think you work too hard."

"I don't think most people think that being an assistant pastor is work."

"On top of your full-time job, it's a lot of mental stress. I think playing this afternoon was good for you." She grinned at him. "I think if I had to do it over again, I'd fall into the water on purpose. That brought out your playful side. I liked it."

He straightened and put an arm on her leg just above her knee. "I definitely liked it. Not the playing exactly, although that was fun, but what came before."

There. He told her he liked to hold her. Her eyes still held a smile and a little bit of tease. "I liked it too."

So much of life was doing things he didn't want to do.

He pushed up from the couch and offered her his hand. "I need to throw my shoes on, then I'm ready to take you home."

"Sounds good." Putting her hand in his, she allowed him to pull her up. He let go immediately and went for his shoes before he was tempted to push for too much.

CAN I WALK YOU HOME tonight?

Blair stood at the back of the sanctuary, fingering her phone. She'd talked to Mrs. Hudson as she'd taken Tinsley home, nodded at the last parishioners as they left, and now she waited for Deacon to get done talking to the last lingering worshiper.

He'd wanted to walk home with her last week too, but he got tied up with board members who wanted an update on Lynette and Pastor Wyatt.

Deacon had just announced from the pulpit that he'd heard from Pastor this afternoon that Lynette was doing better and they would be home sometime this week.

Blair had picked up on some whispers and talking in the church as people wondered what to do about Pastor Wyatt and whether Deacon's position should be elevated to something that was paid. It looked like

Miss Lynette would be in treatments for at least six months. And there was no guarantee that things would get better or easier.

Her heart twirled as she watched Deacon talking seriously with the man and woman standing in front of him. He seemed to have a cloud of calmness all around him. It was something that drew people to him and eased their spirits. She couldn't blame them for wanting to linger.

She'd barely talked to Deacon all week. She'd been busy shoeing horses and taking care of her mother. She didn't think her life would be that crazy once things got settled, but it had been several weeks since the previous farrier had been able to work, and things were backed up.

Not to mention, because of Wilder's position in the horse world, people were hearing about her and calling her. She wouldn't lack for work here.

If only her mother were doing better, the future would look bright.

Especially with Deacon wanting to walk her home, though it made his night even longer.

Deacon finished up his conversation with the couple, and Blair smiled at them as they walked past her.

"I just have to turn off some lights and check to make sure everything's shut down. Are you ready?"

"Yes."

A few minutes later, he locked the front door behind them and took her hand, walking beside her down the sidewalk lit by streetlamps.

Things were mostly deserted, but they walked in silence, enjoying the summer night air.

"How's your job going?" Deacon finally asked when they were just a couple blocks away from her mother's house.

"It's going well. You can probably feel my calluses. I don't exactly have soft hands." She was a little embarrassed about them. But he'd never said anything. She didn't think that was something that bothered Deacon, but she did have a little bit of feminine vanity.

"I love your hands. I love holding them. And I love it when you touch me." He snorted, and she remembered holding his foot and taking the splinter out. "Maybe I shouldn't have admitted that."

"I'm glad you did. I'll remember it."

"I knew Wilder would treat you well and would also spread the word, if he liked the job that you did. You'll have more work than you can handle."

"I almost already do. I need to spend time with my mom. But I need to make enough money to pay the bills too."

She reached across with her hand and touched his arm, running her fingers down his forearm. "How are things going with you? I know you've been really busy working a full-time job and farming and still trying to take over all of Pastor Wyatt's duties and do your own." She stopped for a moment, then said softly, "You look tired."

There was worry in her voice, and she couldn't help it. He was doing too much. She wanted to suggest he let one of those things go, but which one?

"They're gonna vote soon on whether or not they're going to start to pay me. That will be helpful, and I might be able to cut back my hours at the mill." He brushed his hand over her fingers on his arm. "My brothers help me on the farm. This time of year, the work is general maintenance and making sure things are ready for harvest. Although I need to order seed for the cover crop for this fall. I've been forgetting about that. And I need to take some time to sit down and do the paperwork. That always seems to be a drain."

His voice sounded tired and strained, and she wasn't sure it was all about working either. Being a pastor was stressful mentally, because he heard a lot of people's problems.

"How's Mrs. Manarae?" She'd been in the hospital with kidney failure. A longtime member of the church, she taught Sunday school alongside Blair's mom, and Blair remembered her vividly from her youth.

His shoulders slumped, and his face became even more lined. "I should probably go see her tonight. They called the family yesterday, but she pulled through. It's just a matter of time. I'll definitely be going tomorrow after work."

They'd reached the steps of her mom's porch, and Blair stopped. "I'd like to invite you in, but I don't think I should. Your shift starts at four... I assume you're getting up at three, and you need your rest."

He pressed his lips together and looked over her shoulder. "More than all of those other things, I want to spend time with you. It's been hard all week, thinking I might have time to come here and then having something come up. I wanted to be with you every day."

"I wanted you here. Or wanted to be with you. Whatever."

He grinned. "That helps my heart."

"Really? Like you even wondered about that."

"I did. I know absence is supposed to make the heart grow fonder and all that, but absence just makes me wonder what you're doing and if you changed your mind about me."

"I haven't changed my mind. How could I?"

"We never really established what you thought to begin with."

It wasn't a question exactly, but he was fishing for answers, and she didn't know what to say. So she opened her mouth and let her heart come out. "I think there's not another man anywhere who could compare to you. In any way. I want to be with you, and I admire you and wish that I could be worthy of you."

"Stop that already. There's no such thing as being worthy of me. I'm just a sinner saved by grace same as you. No better."

Maybe he thought that way. But the rest of the town didn't. And she had to agree with them. She wasn't good enough to be standing here on her front porch in the dark with Deacon, having him whisper pretty words to her and actually mean them.

"You asked how I felt. That's how."

"I'm falling in love with you. That's how I feel."

Her heart jerked, and her stomach clenched and twisted. She forgot to breathe as Deacon tugged on her hand, pulling her around to face him and bringing her closer. "I wanted to kiss you tonight. That wasn't the whole reason I wanted to walk you home, because I haven't seen you in forever, and I just want to spend time with you. But I thought about that moment in the creek all week long, and I feel like I let an opportunity go by. Life is short, and I don't want to live another week wondering whether I'll get the chance again."

"That's the moment that's played over and over in my mind all week too." She could hardly get the words out, but she thought he deserved to know.

"Good to hear it." His hand touched her arm, and she shivered. "I hope that was a good shiver."

"It was." She put her hands on his waist. Felt the jolt that went through him when she touched him. She couldn't help but smile.

"You like that," he said, with a self-depreciating smile.

"Does it make me wicked that I do?"

"Not wicked. Powerful to me. Honestly, it's a little scary."

"For me too. No one's ever treated me this well, and it feels too good to be true."

"You deserve to be treated this way. Better. Things are so crazy for me right now, but I should be treating you better. I wish..."

She put a hand on his chest and shook her head. "This is the plan God has for us. All the circumstances around us are exactly what He wants us to be in."

"I know that." He grunted. "I could use the reminder, because I want everything else to just go away, and all I need and want is you."

"For right now, that can't be true."

"Then we can pretend."

"If that's what it takes. Or we can just enjoy."

"That sounds better. I like your way." His hand slid up her back and under the hair at her neck. She closed her eyes, thinking it couldn't get any better.

He tugged her closer, and her hands curved around his back, feeling the ridges of ribs and the indentation of his backbone.

"You never said if it was okay for me to kiss you." His voice was husky and soft. A question lingering on the night air.

"That's the best idea I've heard in a long time." She opened her eyes enough to watch his head lower.

Back when she was younger, she'd kissed a lot of men. Maybe she would have said she was good at it. She could also say different men kiss differently, but the end result was pretty much the same.

Deacon's kiss wasn't anything like any of the other kisses she'd ever had.

That shouldn't surprise her, since being with Deacon had been different than being with any other man. Or maybe there was just something about a kiss from a man who respected her and was more concerned about her than him.

That concern for her deepened her desire to please him. Not just in kissing, but with what she could do, because she didn't want to be the taker in the relationship. If he was always giving and making her feel respected and loved, and she wasn't giving the same things as much or more back, then she wasn't doing right by him.

She loved how the better he treated her, the better she wanted to treat him—the way it made her better and made the two of them better together.

Deacon was the same with anyone. He would always give more than he needed to and more than was expected, and he would never expect anything in return.

There were people who would take advantage of that. Just in the short time she'd been in Cowboy Crossing, she'd seen it. But when he did that for her, it made her want to give back. Ask herself what more could she do for him? She bet her doing more for him would inspire him to do more for her, and the upward spiral would make their relationship a beautiful thing.

As long as she didn't mess it up.

It bothered her a little that Deacon had made the first move. But she made a mental note to think about it later, because she could apply the concept that Deacon lived so beautifully to any relationship.

Although the idea of giving and loving so freely was scary.

Deacon looked quiet and serious, but under that veneer beat a heart of courage. One that wasn't afraid to throw itself out and risk the pain of rejection, disappointment, and disdain.

So when he lowered his head, after giving her the beautiful words that she somehow needed to hear, she met him more than halfway and put her whole body and self into kissing the man in front of her and hoping he could tell how much he'd inspired her to change for the better and how much she loved and admired him for it.

Despite all those other kisses she'd shared with all those other men, the world had never spun like this before, her nerve endings had never buzzed, her brain had never shut down so completely that all she could do was hold on to Deacon and kiss him back.

The porch light came on, but it was several more seconds before Deacon lifted his head slowly. Her lips wanted to cling to his, her hands were still on the back of his neck, her body still pushing closer.

Neither of them spoke, and no sound came from the house. After about ten seconds, the porch light went off.

It was a little while after that before Deacon said, "I guess your mom's not in bed."

"I guess not," she said with a wobbly smile.

"I've never been caught making out on the front porch with a girl before."

His words dampened some of the euphoric glow that seemed to emanate from her. She backed up, looking down. "I have."

His hands tightened. "No. Please. Don't go. Not yet. Let me just hold you for a minute. I probably won't see you again until Wednesday, and I don't want to face the next three days, which feel like an eternity, without you."

She moved back into his arms, closing her eyes and leaning her head against his shoulder. If only the world was this simple. As simple as her standing in the strong arms of a good man, falling in love with him.

They stayed like that for a long time before Deacon stirred. "I don't want to let you go, but I know that your mom needs to go to bed."

She tried to keep the worry out of her tone. "So do you. I know you're doing what you love, and I admire that and I respect it, but I wish you'd take care of yourself, too."

"I think she cares about me." His hand came up and touched her cheek.

"I do. Of course I do."

"I definitely care about you too. Probably more than that. Maybe we can talk about that some other time. You go on in the house. I'll wait until I hear the door lock behind you."

"Good night," she said as she stepped reluctantly out of his arms, not wanting to hold him up any longer.

"Good night."

Chapter 17

"Good to see you home, Gus." Deacon settled into the chair across from Pastor Wyatt's desk. The only time he called Pastor Wyatt Gus was when there was no one around. Just to show respect.

"I can't tell you how good it is to be home. It's good to have the children back with us and a little bit of a sense of normalcy."

Deacon leaned forward. "How bad is it, really?"

Gus's eyes dropped to his desk, and his hand clutched the pencil that lay there. "It's bad. But she's been doing well, and they said she could come home as long as her numbers stay good. We have a whole list of things to look for, and if she has any of the symptoms or a bad blood test, we will need to go back immediately. They told us that her cancer is not responsive to chemo. So she's in the trial."

"God is the great physician, and I know that there are people all over the country praying for you."

"I know. Hopefully it's the Lord's will, and she'll be completely healed. I have no idea what I would do without her. I had plenty of time to think about that in the hospital..." His voice trailed off before he raised his head. "She does so much. From schooling the children, taking care of the home, all of the things she does in the church..." He pursed his lips. "She makes me look good. If the church is growing, if people are happy here, if they look at my family and see anything good, it's more because of my wife than me." The pencil twirled in his hand. "All day every day without complaining. She's homeschooling the children right now. From the couch if necessary."

Deacon could have told Gus that a long time ago. Everyone knew that Lynette worked tirelessly without stopping to make her husband look good. She lived the Bible principle of putting others first. Her children had an amazing example to look up to. Even if her husband wasn't always appreciative and maybe at times didn't even notice, she could rest assured that God did.

Maybe now, if she pulled through, Gus would be more appreciative, since his eyes had been opened to what she did.

Deacon hoped he never took advantage of his wife like that. Or anyone else. Christians were easy to take advantage of, the ones who were living right, because they would do for you without ever asking for or expecting anything in return. One had a tendency to start thinking that they deserved it, instead of being grateful.

Or to think they were weak because they gave without expecting anything in return.

Lack of character on the part of the receiver and an excess of character on the part of someone who continued to give as God commanded.

"Deacon, I know you probably know this is coming, but I've had a lot of people calling me while I've been away."

Deacon leaned back in the chair and set one ankle on his knee. Relaxed. He had a pretty good idea of what Gus was going to say. Blair's face flashed through his mind, the way it looked last night after he kissed her.

Don't ask me to give that up. Please, God.

"I haven't been here much since Blair came back." Gus steepled his fingers and leveled a look at Deacon. "She does have a reputation. You need to be careful. I trust you. I know you'll do right, and I have your back, but I can't manipulate the board."

He figured Gus would stand by him, but he hadn't been sure. "I appreciate that. I don't expect you to fight the board for me, but I do appreciate you standing beside me about it."

"While we're talking about it, can we clarify exactly what 'it' is? What's going on between you two?"

"I love her. I'll marry her as soon as she'll have me."

"Does she know that? How does she feel?"

"I haven't told her that. No. It's only been a month. I think these things usually go a little slower than that?"

Gus smiled, acknowledging that Deacon was right. "I'm sorry. Time slipped away from me. It could have been one day or could have been one hundred years since Lynette was diagnosed with cancer. It feels the same."

"I'm sorry I'm making your return harder. I didn't mean to be one of your problems."

"No. Not you. But we do have one loud voice on the board, who has called me at least ten times, complaining. Most of the rest of the board is in favor of taking you on as a salaried employee and putting you in my position if I have to go. But that one loud voice has several other people wavering, and a decision has to be a two-thirds majority."

"It's in God's hands. I'm fine with that."

"You could back off with Blair. Just for a bit. It's not going to solve all your problems, but it will get you voted in for now." Gus paused. "I'm sure she knows how much better you are than her and would be willing to sacrifice a bit to help you."

Deacon's foot hit the floor with a thud. "I won't sit here and listen to that. I'm not any better than anyone else, and I'm certainly not any better than Blair. I—"

"I'm sorry." Gus held his hands up. "That came out badly. I shouldn't have said it like that." His hands dropped back down to his desk. "You could still consider breaking up for a bit."

"No. I'm not going to pretend something I don't feel. Or pretend to not feel something I do. Not when there's nothing wrong with it. I've waited all my life for God to bring the right woman in. Waited." He had to emphasize that word. "I'm not going to act like there's something wrong with the way I feel about Blair, and I'm definitely not going to act like there's something wrong with *her*. She's done nothing but good since she's come."

Gus was listening, and Deacon kept talking. "Everyone has things in their past. Including that board member you are talking about. If I recall correctly, about the time Blair was having her wild days, he was too. Only Blair got caught, and he didn't."

"He had a good family too. That always helps." Pastor steepled his hands and tapped his two pointer fingers together. "I don't blame you. If I had to choose between Lynette and being a pastor, I would choose Lynette. God made that bond to be strong for a reason. Families have to be strong, because they carry the country, and the world, on their shoulders. We've weakened them and made it okay for them not to be what God wants. That's to everyone's detriment. Blair's a casualty of that."

Deacon had to agree. Mike, the board member who was causing all the problems, had run in Blair's crowd. In the time Deacon had spent with her, Blair hadn't said a word about him, although she had to have heard that he'd complained loudly and long about her.

It made Deacon think that maybe there were some things that Mike didn't want the church to know, and he was afraid Blair might tell them.

He made a mental note to talk to Blair about him, even if she didn't want to. He hated talking to her about those things, because she already felt like she wasn't good enough. Funny the difference between her and Mike, who not only felt like he was good enough despite his past, but he was on the board.

"There's nothing we can do. I just would have been remiss if I hadn't said something to you. I'm sure you've heard the whispers and the rumors."

"And the outright complaints. People haven't been shy to tell me to my face that she doesn't deserve to teach and that I shouldn't be hanging around her." He pulled a lip back. "Not everyone."

Anger at people being unwilling to forgive and forget pressed in his chest. It wasn't like she was currently sinning. She'd been hurt by her past, but had moved away from it and was trying to limp into a new life, letting the old things go.

It almost made him ashamed to be a Christian. Christians were the only group of people that killed their wounded.

"It doesn't matter how many times I say the church is a hospital for sinners, people just don't get it." Gus tapped the eraser against the open iPad that sat on his desk. "Some of them are justified. They want good examples for their children in leadership positions. I can't blame them for that, and the Bible does have stipulations. I get it." He set the pencil down carefully. "You can love the sinner and hate the sin, and you can do it graciously. Some people just don't."

It hurt Deacon's heart that people would say unkind things about Blair and hurt it even worse that she would say that she deserved them.

Gus continued. "Forgiveness is something we strive for. I'm not sure those people mean to be unkind. But they're forgetting that the church is a hospital. The people here that are saying those unkind things about Blair need the same kind of treatment from you and me that we want them to give to others, including Blair. They're hurting just as much. And they need grace just as much."

Deacon nodded. It was true. He did have a tendency to complain about the loudmouths who caused problems, but the loudmouths needed love too.

A few beats of silence passed before Gus shifted. "All right then. I have some other things I wanted to talk to you about. We have a wedding coming up soon."

"Yeah. Chandler and Ivory. It's not going to be a fancy affair, although everybody from the church has been invited. I'm glad you and Lynette are home and can hopefully make it."

"And the reception is out at your parents' house, correct?"

"Sure is. If it rains, it will be in the equipment shed. But this time of year, things are usually pretty dry."

"You've been doing marriage counseling with them?"

"Yep. They did really well. I think they're going to be good." Deacon nodded, thinking about his brother, and the way Ivory made him a better man, and how Ivory had blossomed under the love and attention that Chandler had given her. "They've definitely brought out the best in each other. And they're committed to continue."

"Those are the best kind of weddings. I'm looking forward to it."

"Me too."

Chapter 18

Blair got up early Tuesday morning, fed Mr. Rogers, did her devotions, and made breakfast for her mom, who had been getting up earlier and seeming to do better. But when she wasn't up ten minutes before Blair needed to leave for work, she ran up the stairs and knocked on her bedroom door. There was no answer.

She knocked harder, thinking that she didn't have a very big workload today and might get off early. She'd be able to shop for groceries. She wasn't going to be able to slip in a meeting with Deacon, though. He'd texted her late last night and told her that Lynette had taken a turn for the worse, and Pastor Wyatt was taking her back to the hospital in St. Louis.

Deacon had said he was taking a day off work and going out with him, just to be there. It was a discouraging setback.

So there was no hope of her seeing Deacon today. She wasn't exactly depressed, but she didn't look at the sunshine and the beautiful day with quite as much eagerness as she would if there was a chance.

Thankfully she and her mother had been developing a better relationship. Ever since they went out to the diner together, and Blair had apologized, and she and her mother talked, they'd been feeling their way into a closer and deeper relationship.

Blair had to admit coming home had been the best thing she'd ever done. She still had her apartment that she needed to go clean out and close up, but she had until the end of the month.

She knocked again on the door, harder than last time, and called out, "Mom? Mom? It's time to get up. I need to go to work."

Still no response.

She tried the door handle. It turned under her hand, so she pushed the door open.

Blair took two steps into the room. Her mom lay on the bed, on her back, with her hands crossed over her chest.

It was a position Blair had seen before. It put her in mind of a corpse in a funeral casket.

The thought made her whole body go cold. Her legs buckled. She caught herself before she fell to the floor and slowly walked to the foot of the bed.

She didn't have to touch the cold, stiff foot of her mother to know that her mother had met Jesus last night.

At that thought, she did fall to her knees beside the bed, gripping her mother's foot, waiting for the sobs that were backed up in her throat and her chest and her heart, wishing they would come out, but unable to cry. Unable to do anything but hold onto her mother's foot and stare at the floor and wish that she'd had more time.

TWO WEEKS LATER

Blair stood off to the side as the wedding guests slowly made their way through the bridal line and out of the church. They would be heading toward the Hudsons' property, where food for the adults and games for the children awaited.

She'd heard about the wedding planning progress each time she'd been in church, since Mrs. Hudson had made a point to talk to her about it.

Blair had never been to a wedding reception where the children changed into swimming suits and played water games, but apparently that was what was happening this afternoon.

Blair wouldn't be there.

Two weeks ago, when she found her mother, she took that as a sign from the Lord. Her mother was the reason that she'd come back.

She'd made her peace with her, and all it had taken to make up her mind about leaving now that she'd accomplished what she'd come for was the phone call she'd received later that afternoon.

Someone from the church had blamed her for her mother's death and said it was her wild past and the sin in her life that had caused her mother to get sick and die. That person also said that she needed to back off and leave Deacon alone so that he could carry on the work of the Lord and not have her sin affect his ministry too.

She'd given her two-week notice to Wilder Stryker that evening.

The next days were a blur. She'd picked out a casket and made the arrangements, decided to take Mr. Rogers and Rascal with her and talked to Deacon, who didn't understand why she had pulled away from him.

She could see it in his eyes and the slope of his shoulders and his curled hands as he reached out for her and she turned away.

The pain in her heart from losing her mom was harsh, but the pain in her heart from hurting Deacon was almost more than she could bear. It made her want to double up and curl into herself and squeeze in somewhere tight and dark and deserted and just hurt alone.

But she'd gone back to work by Thursday, and she did what she was supposed do.

Deacon was busy with two funerals, because Mrs. Manarae, with the kidney failure, had died as well. With Pastor Wyatt gone and Lynette worsening, Deacon had his hands full.

Although, with the wedding, today was a happy day.

Hopefully, when she told Deacon her car was packed, and she was leaving Cowboy Crossing for good instead of going to the reception, he'd be okay. It had been almost two weeks since their unbelievable kiss. They'd barely talked.

She'd ignored his texts as well as his calls, and when he pressed her about it for a few seconds at church, she'd just said she needed time to get over her mother's death.

Which was true.

But she couldn't stay here, couldn't have a relationship with him, without him finding out about Tinsley, and there were more worms in that can. She didn't want to open it.

Part of her thought maybe she was making the wrong decision, but the biggest part saw what she was doing as the plan for her life. She knew Deacon was too good for her, and everyone else in town knew it too.

Or maybe, it was just she wanted to go back to where she came from. Where there were no phone calls telling her she killed her mother and would ruin the man she loved. Where she was building a life and no one knew her past, no one held it in front of her face, expecting her to live down to their low expectations instead of encouraging her to do better. That she could do better.

That she *was* better.

It was what she needed to do.

It was not what she wanted to do.

She'd watched as Tinsley skipped out of the church, giving her uncle a high five and Ivory, who looked absolutely stunning and radiant in her white gown with lace trim, a hug.

From where he stood with his brother, Deacon had looked at Blair several times and tried to make his way to her twice. Both times, he'd been stopped by someone who wanted to talk. She stood waiting.

Something tugged on her arm, and Blair looked down.

"Are you coming to the reception? Grandma wants to know if you want to ride with us?" Tinsley asked.

Blair looked down into the eyes of her daughter. Innocent eyes. Eyes that had been sheltered and protected and encouraged and taught character and morality and justice. Eyes of a little girl who would grow to be a fine woman with the best father in the world.

Only Mrs. Hudson knew her secret, and she'd kept it like she'd said.

Would she keep it even after Blair was gone?

Probably. Mrs. Hudson was an honorable woman and had said she wouldn't tell.

"Thank you so much for offering. Tell your grandma I said thank you, but I'm going to talk to your dad for a minute before I leave here."

There. She managed not to promise to be there, and to not lie, while also not telling the truth. Guilt tugged at her insides along with a longing which wrapped around her heart and lungs and ribs like a boa constrictor.

"Okay." Tinsley twirled to leave but then twirled back around. "If you bring your swimsuit, you can swim with us. We're going to play in the water."

"I'll remember that," Blair said, blinking to keep her eyes from watering.

Tinsley skipped away and bounced out the side door. Blair watched her go, wishing, longing, that things could have been different.

Taking a deep breath through her nose, she turned, and Deacon strode up.

"You look at my daughter like you love her."

"Doesn't everyone?" Blair deflected the comment.

Deacon let it go. "How are you holding up?"

She straightened her shoulders and tried to keep her expression cool. "I'm fine. I had enough casseroles in the freezer to feed me all winter."

He laughed. "That's what Baptists do best. Send food. All homemade of course."

"Of course." Inez had already come and took the casseroles to her house. With all her children, she could use every one.

Deacon tilted his head. "I've been kind of thinking that you've been avoiding me. But I've been busy. So maybe it's just bad timing, although you didn't come to the rehearsal last night. You were invited."

"I had some things I needed to do."

His brows went up, but he didn't say anything. In the silence hung the question: what in the world could she have had to do that could have been more important than the wedding rehearsal and seeing the man that she'd been kissing on her porch two weeks ago?

Deacon lowered his voice, and his words came out strained. "I want to help you. If I can't help you, I just want to be with you. Is that too much?"

He'd been amazing leading the wedding service. He'd done a beautiful job on the ceremony and when speaking for a few minutes on the subject of love. Words that were timeless and applicable and beautiful and inspiring. He'd been confident and funny, serious and at ease. She'd admired him as always as she watched.

Now he stood in front of her, wanting her.

She crossed her arms over her chest. "I know there's a vote coming up in the church, and they don't want you if you're with me." The words didn't want to come, but she forced them out anyway. "I'm not any good for you."

"That's not—"

She held her hand up. "Wait. Let me speak."

He clamped his mouth closed, but his fingers stretched and fisted at his sides.

"Everything that you've done for me has made me want to be a better person. You've accepted me and given of yourself to me without asking anything in return. From inviting me into your family, to giving me the reference to the job that I got, to the beautiful words and amazing kiss." His face contracted; she shook her head. "The whole time, we knew that we wouldn't work out. You and me. There are just too many complicated things in my past, and I would always be afraid of them coming out."

Deacon spread his hand out, his voice low and almost pleading. "The hard stuff is already out. Everyone already knows what you've done. Now they can see who you are. The woman that you are now. Not the kid you were then."

"Some things are too precious to risk."

An angry voice interrupted them, startling Blair. "I thought we talked to you about this. I thought I told you that if you continued to see her, I wasn't going to be able to vote for you, and you won't have the two-thirds majority that you need in order to get paid. We'll run you out of this church." Mike stood on her left, and Blair turned her head. The church was far from empty, and people milled around, closer and closer, curious about the confrontation going on in the corner.

Deacon didn't even turn his head. His eyes were staring into hers. She could hardly stand the pain in them. He knew she was saying goodbye, and he didn't understand.

She didn't know what to say to make him understand. She didn't want to hurt him. That had never been her intention.

"What things?" he asked in a soft voice, pain lacing his words. "Tell me what things. We'll get rid of them. We don't have to keep anything. Just us."

She swallowed, thinking that she had been all cried out from losing her mom, and the funeral, and the decisions that she made, but realizing that that wasn't the slightest bit true as her eyes pricked and tears filled them. She wasn't going to have a choice. He wasn't going to understand until she told the truth.

She shook her head, unable to get any words out.

"Are you talking about Tinsley? Are you talking about the fact that you're her mother?" he asked.

Her eyes grew big, and she gasped. "How?"

Mike's voice interrupted them. "Ha. I should have known you weren't such a goody-goody." He hit Deacon on the arm. "Back in the day, she'd sleep with anyone." He grunted. "So you're the unlucky idiot who ended up being the father of her kid."

That was too much for Blair. She knew it was a wedding, and she wanted to be respectful, but she wouldn't tolerate the smear on Deacon's character. That was exactly what she was trying to avoid. "No, you jerk," she said in a voice loud enough to quiet the church. "You fathered Tinsley."

She whirled around, moving out of Deacon's grasp as his hand came up to hold her. "I already gave my two-week notice two weeks ago. I'm leaving. I'm going back to the town where I came from, where they don't know my past and they don't know what I've done. Where I don't have to see my daughter every day and know that she can never be mine. You know the Lord closed the door on Cowboy Crossing when my mother died."

"Maybe that was an open door," Deacon said fiercely.

She stared at him, never having thought of that. Death was always a closed door.

"Maybe that was to push you out of your wallowing in self-pity. Did you not see all of the people at your mother's funeral? How they loved her? How she'd done so much good in her life? Didn't you see the doors opening in front of you and all that could be yours if you just walk through them? You don't even have to do so with me. Just do it." His voice had strengthened, but pain still tightened his face. "And you should be a part of your daughter's life."

"I'm not the dad," Mike said angrily, ignoring their conversation.

Deacon turned to him. "No, you're not. I am."

Blair spun and power-walked out of the church. It was too much. She couldn't process it all. She had everything all planned out in a nice, tidy package, and Deacon came in and shot holes through all of her faulty reasoning, making more sense than she ever could.

And what had she done?

She'd just walked out, embarrassing him in front of the man on the board who wanted to get rid of him.

Another question bothered her more.

How had Deacon found out about Tinsley?

If Mrs. Hudson had told him, Blair was going to lose a lot of respect for her, since she'd said she wasn't going to. It wasn't her secret to tell.

She stepped off the sidewalk and started walking to her car when the thought hit her.

What was she doing?

The man wanted her. He made no bones about it. What made her decide that she wasn't good enough for him when he thought she was?

He didn't look at her and see all of her past mistakes. Or maybe that wasn't quite true. Maybe he saw all of her past mistakes, and he loved her anyway.

What he'd said just a few minutes ago as he married Ivory and Chandler came back to her. When he'd been talking about putting others first. About esteeming them better than herself. About how that wasn't directly applied to a marriage in Scriptures, but how it was the duty of every Christian, and why would they not do that in the relationship that was closest to them?

Deacon had done that with her. He'd not questioned whether or not she was worthy of love; he just loved her. He had looked at her and saw someone that he was better than, but in lowliness of mind, he'd esteemed her better than himself.

While she had put herself and her fears first. She'd thought he was helping her become a better person, and maybe he was, but her old self had come to the forefront here in this decision.

Turning in mid-stride, she started marching right back into that church.

She yanked the door open in time to see the entire board gathered around Deacon and Mike.

Someone was talking, but when Deacon saw her walk back in, he broke out of the group and walked over to her.

He reached out for her. "I—"

She shook her head. "Me. I need to apologize first." She lowered her head. "I'm sorry. I'm an idiot. I might still have trouble and not always remember this, but you're right. You've shown me what true love is, and I haven't wanted to believe you because the idea is so preposterous. That someone would just love me, no matter what I am. I can't even believe it."

"Jesus. He loves you like that."

"And I saw Jesus in you. Because that's how you love me."

"I don't think I've told you that I loved you. How did you figure it out?"

"Because of the way you act. You *showed* me love. You were love with boots on. You didn't need to say it."

"Well, I'm going to." His eyes stared into hers. "I love you. I was already falling in love with you, and a few weeks ago when I was changing my clothes upstairs at my parents' house and heard through the heat vent what you were saying to my mom about being Tinsley's mom, everything fell into place for me. I already loved you, but that solidified everything."

Blair's heart raced, although she also felt free and light, like she could float.

Of course. He'd overheard. Mrs. Hudson hadn't told him. Of course not.

"I want us to be a family. I don't want to push too hard. But that's what I want. With you."

"What about them?" She nodded over his shoulder at the board members that were standing behind him.

"I think it's going to go in my favor, but even if it doesn't, I don't care. There's no doubt in my mind that you're the one that God has for me. And if that means tribulation at church, then that's what it means."

"Are you sure?" Her brows scrunched together, and she looked up at him.

"Dead sure."

He lowered his head and kissed her, and she knew then that she was the most blessed woman in the world, because she had a man like this for the rest of her life.

Epilogue

"I now pronounce you man and wife. You may kiss the bride." Pastor Wyatt's face may have aged ten years since his wife was diagnosed with cancer, but it wreathed into a smile as he looked at Blair and Deacon.

Pastor Wyatt had secured a teaching position in St. Louis, but he'd come back specifically to marry the new pastor of Cowboy Crossing just before Thanksgiving.

Loyal Hudson watched the wedding, via his computer and the web cam Chandler had set up, with bittersweet emotions, carefully controlled.

He had not planned to be single and alone in his thirties.

He had also not planned to lose a child in a house fire, which made the loss of half of his face and the other physical defects saving his other child from the fire had caused, not such a big deal.

Except it was.

His wife had fallen in love with the doctor who'd overseen their surviving child's recovery, taking that child with her when she left him for the doc and leaving Loyal facing the rest of his life – a grotesque shell of the man he'd been – alone. Hardly hoping, with his face – and admittedly, his attitude as well – for a second chance at love.

His wife had no lingering physical effects from the fire. How could she? She hadn't been there when it started. She'd been in a hotel room in Trumball – the bigger town to their east – with a guy she'd met through her job as a consultant for the big company she worked for.

Lord? I was faithful. I thought you rewarded the faithful.

Sitting here watching Deacon and Blair's happiness didn't feel like a reward. It felt like torture, although he was certainly happy for his brother. Deacon deserved a good woman.

If there was such a thing.

Loyal shouldn't be so bitter. He'd managed to buy into an ag company that had caught the emerging hemp market on the upswing, make a boatload of cash while growing the company into an international force, then selling before hemp crashed and burned, like ag markets always did.

He'd walked away a rich man.

A rich, lonely, bitter man.

He'd bought the company and did most of the work before the fire, selling it from his hospital bed while he'd been recuperating from his burns.

It had been a long recuperation. But, finally, now he was as good as he could be, and he was ready to go after his ex for joint custody.

He looked around his state-of-the-art kitchen from his position on the end bar stool. He'd used some of his money to cater to the hobby he'd had since he was a child – cooking. He hoped that was something that could bring him and his daughter back together. She'd cried and refused to stay with him the three times his ex had brought her to visit since the fire.

Loyal had given up for a while, but he wasn't giving up on his daughter. She was all he had left. He would entice her by spending time in the kitchen with her.

That, and riding horses on the farm. She'd always loved that when she was a baby.

Deacon and Blair had disappeared from his screen after sharing a loving kiss and a look that said far more about how they felt about each other than the kiss had. Loyal shoved the uncomfortable knot of longing down out of his throat and brushed a hand over the cool granite of his countertop.

Maybe he should have gone to his brother's wedding. Of course he should have. But Deacon understood why he didn't. Maybe once he had a few more years to get used to his scarred face and the stares of everyone he met.

He was closing his computer as his phone rang. Pulling it from his back pocket, he saw that it was Chandler before he answered. "Yeah?"

"Hey, man. You watch it?"

"Yeah. It was a wedding."

"Pretty sweet."

Loyal didn't say anything. It *was* sweet. Bittersweet for him.

"Hey, you remember all those nights I spent in the hospital with you, and how I twisted the doctor's arms to send your daughter from St. Louis to the burn specialist unit in Chicago, and how that probably saved her after the infection that moved thought the burn ward after she left-"

"Yeah, yeah. Obviously you want something. Spit it out."

"I have a friend who needs a country kitchen to film a few episodes of her cooking show. Since you owed me for all those things I just mentioned, plus, I did handle some of the attorney's paperwork on your business transaction-"

"No."

"Too late. I already told her yes. The film crew is arriving next week – just a small crew – camera guys, a director and my friend, Madeline, the...chef."

Odd the way he stumbled over the world "chef." But the answer came easily. "No."

Of all the things he didn't want, a film crew in his house was on the very top of the list, occupying slots one, two and three on that particular list.

"They're making a donation to the burn center in St. Louis in memory of Dyer. And they're dedicating the first show to him."

Loyal leaned his elbows on the cold counter, his head down, his heart wrenching painfully as his stomach gummed up in a convoluted mess. Dyer was the son he hadn't been able to save.

"I don't want them underfoot."

"They won't be. Madeline will probably stay there, so she won't be mobbed in town, but the rest of the crew will stay in Trumball."

Since Chandler had been a big movie star, Loyal understood about rabid fans, so he got that the woman, whoever she was – he didn't even own a tv – would want to stay here...but he didn't have to like it. Still, he just couldn't be any more of a jerk about it than he'd already been. Chandler really had been good to him when he'd been laid up.

"Madeline is a big name, but she's not a snob. She might help you with Nicole," Chandler said, knowing Loyal's weakness was his daughter. "If you refuse to take payment for the use of your house – you don't need it anyway – you might make a deal where she spends so much time with Nicole or something."

Yeah, Loyal could see the possibilities. Maybe he could do something to mess with his ex. She'd lorded things over him for so long...he could definitely use Madeline's gratitude to work some things in his favor, as long as he could do it away from the cameras, and preferably, away from Madeline's eyes as well.

If she were a celebrity, she'd be beautiful, which was the last, the very last, type of person he wanted to be around.

Still, there were possibilities and he intended to use them to his advantage. He also intended to win back the heart of his daughter, who was the only female in the world, aside from maybe his mother, that he would ever care about again.

THANKS SO MUCH FOR reading!

The Beast Gets His Cowgirl in the Show Me State is next in the series.

Reviews are welcome and appreciated!

Printed in Great Britain
by Amazon